BREATHING UNDERWATER

BREATHING UNDERWATER

Julia Green

GALAXY

PLUS

First published in Great Britain in 2009 by
Bloomsbury Publishing plc
This Large Print edition published 2010
by BBC Audiobooks
by arrangement with
Bloomsbury Publishing plc

ISBN: 978 1405 663663

Lines from the poem 'Fern Hill' by
Dylan Thomas are from *The Poems* by Dylan
Thomas, published by J M Dent. Reproduced by
permission of
David Higham Associates

Line from the poem 'Not Waving But Drowning' by
Stevie Smith is from *Selected Poems* by Stevie Smith,
published by Penguin Books Ltd, 1978. Reproduced
by permission of the Estate of James MacGibbon

British Library Cataloguing in Publication Data available

Printed and bound in Great Britain by
CPI Antony Rowe, Chippenham and Eastbourne

For my sisters, Alison and Sue

It starts like this: a sudden storm. Squalls of rain batter my bedroom window, rattling the glass. A shrieking wind shakes the roof slates on the small stone house. A loose slate breaks free, slides and spins down the roof, shatters into tiny pieces on the path below.

I lie in the dark for hours, listening to the storm moan and howl round the house, tugging it as if it's a boat to be torn from its moorings. But the house stands solid, like it's done for nearly a hundred years through storms wilder than this. Finally, at dawn, the wind drops.

Still I can't sleep. I get dressed, go to knock on Joe's bedroom door. The door's ajar. I whisper into the grey light, 'I'm going down the beach. Coming?'

After a storm, there are always things to find. Over the years, people here have scratched a living out of wrecks and stuff washed up. Joe and me have found all sorts.

Joe's already awake. He pulls on jeans and fleece, stumbles downstairs after me. The back door is unlocked, as always. We pull boots on: the rubber's cold on my bare feet. We go the lane way to Periglis, the most westerly of the beaches. Neither of us says much. I'm amazed Joe's come with me, though I don't tell him that. I'm happy now, running ahead. The storm's brought down whole branches: swathes of leaves and twigs clog up the lane. The air is cool, damp: smells like autumn, though it's summer, still. August.

I'm first at the beach. I jump down on to the rocks at the top, almost slip. Everything's shiny and wet. Mist curls off the sea like smoke. The

1

tide's high, just on the turn. I kick through the piled-up stinking weed, and start making a stack of driftwood we can take home to dry. I stop to stretch out my spine. I watch the sea edging back, revealing small patches of fine silver sand.

A little way out, the water seems to be breaking over something large. A low, dark object, like rock, but there are no rocks just there. I wait, watch. A piece of wrecked boat? A seal, perhaps, or a leatherback turtle, like the one washed up on Bryluen two years ago. Sometimes even whales get stranded after a storm.

The sea, like the sky, is milky grey. Quieter now, sighing *in, out*, like breathing. It sucks and rolls the object, draws it back in the running tide. Bit by bit, the sea retreats.

And now I see what it's brought us. Not a seal, or a turtle. Not a beached whale. I gasp, but no sound comes, just a rush of air. There's a bare foot, and then another, in a sodden trainer. Jeans, T-shirt, seaweed hair. The waves roll the heavy figure slightly, pull back. They leave the bloated body belly down on the silver sand and shingle, head twisted awkwardly to one side. I can't stop looking. I stare at the mottled skin of the naked foot, and the bruised cheekbone.

It's weird but I don't feel horror, or fear, or even pity, at that moment. I'm simply curious, seeing something for the first time, like a small child discovering the world.

Joe's behind me. 'What the—!' He clutches my arm. 'Christ, Freya!' He wades out through the shallow water, and with the tip of his boot he turns the head slightly, and I see the face. The boy's mouth is slightly open, like a fish. Eyes shut. His

2

skin is puffy, a strange purple and white colour. I take all this in. I can tell he's been dead a while. A stranger. I watch Joe bend right over the body, touch the face and hand. For just that moment, there's no one else but us in the whole world: Joe and me and a drowned boy.

When Joe stands up, there are tears on his face. I stare, surprised. It's so unlike Joe. The boy is no one we know, and so far beyond our help that I don't feel sad, just sort of tender. And the weirdest thing: to me he seems at peace now, rolled over and over by the waves and laid out on the silver sand in the pearly early morning light. Nothing can hurt him any more.

'Come on. Got to get someone.' Joe tugs my arm, starts running up the beach, back along the path. I take one last look at the boy before I turn and follow Joe.

I'm out of breath, running to catch up. 'I found him first. I want to tell.'

Joe stops and looks at me, suddenly furious. 'What's the matter with you? How can you even think like that? A boy *drowned*, Freya!'

*   *   *

Back at home, we both tell, interrupting each other. Evie and Gramps phone the police and the coastguard; a police boat comes out from Main Island, and soon the beach is swarming with people. The dead boy's not *ours*—mine and Joe's—any longer.

We find out later that the boy's nineteen, a French fisherman, washed overboard days before the storm. The wind and the waves brought him to us. The chances of that happening?

But people drown all the time. One every seventeen hours, in the UK. People get washed off rocks, there are boating accidents. Years ago, sixteen men from this island drowned in one night in a storm: practically the entire male population. Gramps says that some fishermen don't ever learn to swim, on purpose; that way they'll die more quickly if they go overboard. I can't get my head round that. Joe and I both swim like fish.

Joe sticks up a poster in his room: a map showing all the wrecks around the islands. Thousands.

*   *   *

I didn't particularly notice, at the time, how fascinated Joe was with this stuff. He's always had a thing about the sea, danger, stories about disasters. Now I'm beginning to piece things together, I've started to wonder what exactly it meant to Joe, us finding the boy, that morning. Was that where it all started? Or am I making too much of it? Was it just one of those things, a random event, a tragedy for the boy and his family and his friends, somewhere in Brittany, but nothing more significant than that? Not a premonition, not a *foreshadowing* of what came later.

Because that's what you do, when something terrible happens. You go over and over every tiny thing, looking for clues, trying to find a pattern and a way to make sense out of the muddle and hurt. The drowned boy happened the year I was twelve and my brother Joe was fifteen, and a year later, Joe was dead.

4

One

I'm on the train, the start of the journey. It's the first time I've been back to the island since Joe's accident, last summer. It's just me, this time. Mum won't come back *ever*, she says, as if seeing again the place where he died will make things worse. How, exactly? The worst has already happened. The ache of it runs through my body like a seam of coal in rock, black and cold and terrible.

Miranda's mum says *you'd never get over the death of your child.* Miranda told me that yesterday, when we were in my old bedroom in the attic, putting the last of my things into boxes. Downstairs, Mum was packing up pictures and ornaments, ready for the move. We went past her on the landing, on our way down to get drinks in the kitchen. She was lifting down the big gold-framed mirror from its place on the wall. She held the mirror in both hands, staring at her own reflection in the spotted glass. I looked at her face, framed in the mirror like a painting: *Grieving Woman: self-portrait.* She'd tied her hair back with a bit of old string. She was wearing the same sleeveless grey linen dress she's worn all week, so now it was all creased and limp. Ghost-mother. She didn't speak. Didn't notice us, even.

'She still cries at night,' I said to Miranda. 'Even a year on.'

Miranda's mum's words echo in my head. *Never.* That's the worst one. I don't want to believe that it's always going to be like this: Mum silent and sad and distracted; Dad out, or working all the time.

There are lots of different ways grown-ups disappear. It's lonely, being the one left behind.

Now Miranda's in Spain somewhere, with her family, and I'm on my way to the islands, to my favourite place on earth, except that . . . well, it's just me. By myself.

'Are you sure you should go?' Miranda said. 'I know you love it, and everything, but won't it just be too sad? Bring back all the memories?'

But I want to remember. That's the whole point. I want to remember everything, all the tiny details, and I want to work something out. There's this big horrible question mark hanging over it all, about Joe. Gradually, the question's got stronger. I reckon it's what's eating away at Mum, nibbling her from the inside, turning her into a hollow shell.

The question is this. Was it an accident, *really*?

*　　　*　　　*

The train wheels rattle as we go into the first of a series of tunnels through the red cliff. The track goes right next to the sea. As we come out into daylight again, I press my face against the glass. Silvery-blue light reflects off the sea. I want to drink it in, all the light and the colour. For the first time in ages, a little quiver of excitement runs down my spine. Or is it fear?

I've done this journey so many times with Joe, I still can't quite believe he's not here now. Lately, I've had these . . . well, strange things have been happening. Out of the corner of my eye, I glimpse a shadow, a shape. Or the door opens, but no one's there. Sometimes there's a smell, like river water. I haven't told anyone, not even Miranda. I want to

6

see him so much, and I'm terrified, too. Like, he's going to speak. Tell me something. And I know that it sounds ridiculous, and it's impossible, and everything, but I'm scared of what he might tell me.

The train's slowed right down to go over the old iron bridge that spans the wide river in a beautiful curve, so high above the river that when you go across it's almost like flying. If Joe was here, he'd have his head out of the window even though you aren't allowed, and his hair would be wilder than ever, full of tangles that would stay the entire summer and no one would mind. Evie couldn't care less what we look like. She's not your average sort of gran.

I squeeze past the woman in the seat next to mine, out into the swaying carriage and down to the doors. It's one of those long-distance trains where the inside doors are automatic, but you can still pull down the windows on the exit doors. That's what I do. The window sticks, and I have to work it loose, till there's space for me to stick my head right out, like Joe would've done. The wind rushes at my face and makes my eyes water. So much air and space! It's exhilarating after hours stuck inside the stuffy train.

The wind tugs and pulls, as if it wants me to come out further: out, out and then down, down, down—gravity, I suppose, pulling me down to earth. Or down to water, rather, because the river's directly below. For a second I go dizzy. I imagine opening the door, stepping out into air and space and light. I smell estuary mud, salt. Sounds crash back in: creaking train wheels and seagulls screaming, a boat horn; it's like a picture suddenly coming to life. Everything's coming sharply into focus.

That's when it happens.

Joe's voice, in my ear. 'Careful, Freya!'

He's standing right behind me. His hand's on my arm, holding me back from the too-far-open window. For a brief second, relief floods through me. Everything's OK. Nothing has happened after all. He's here. And then a different voice is shouting, and rough hands are pushing past me, yanking up the window.

'Stupid girl! Can't you read? IT IS DANGEROUS TO LEAN OUT OF THE WINDOW.'

Dazed, I shove past the ticket collector, back into the carriage and my seat. My eyes are blurry with tears. I'm shaking all over.

Two

I don't really believe in ghosts. But something must happen after you die. Otherwise, what is the point? It is impossible for me to believe that Joe has just disappeared completely, in an instant. How could someone so alive and funny and maddening and clever and amazing as Joe just vanish? I have thought about this for a whole year, nearly. So what's going on? Am I just imagining what I want to believe? Conjuring him up out of my imagination? Or could it be that because I'm somehow open to the possibility, he can actually come back, in one way or another? What exactly did happen, back there at the door?

I don't believe in the white spectre-type ghosts you get in stories, but what if ghosts are something else? Like memories, somehow caught and trapped in time, released by being in certain places where the things first happened. Or what if dead people can actually come back in some way, a spirit version of themselves, the same way they come in dreams, when you're sleeping?

My heart's thumping like mad. I'm still holding my breath. I let it out, in a long sigh. The woman next to me stares and I look away, quick, out of the window. Moorland, chimneys, the remnants of derelict tin mines. Deep wooded valleys. Mist, turning to drizzle. Another hour to go. I close my eyes, drift into sleep.

Bit by bit, we're edging closer.

The drizzle has turned to rain. Slanting sheets of it hit the train windows, run in rivers down the glass. The train is a column of light snaking through a grey landscape.

I get off the train, find my way to the ferry, find a seat where I can leave my bag, and go up on the deck to watch the crew winding in the mooring ropes, pulling up the huge doors. Just before we leave the harbour, a storm warning comes out over the loudspeakers. They give you the option of delaying your journey. Full refund. No one is to stay out on deck. I go back down below.

The ferry creeps along the coast as far as the tip of the peninsula, then it starts ploughing westwards. The rollers come in one long uninterrupted sweep across the Atlantic: there's nothing between here and America. The ferry begins to pitch and roll. The engines change note. It's going to take hours, having to go so slow. The

9

ferry creaks and groans and a deep *thud* shakes through the whole ship each time an extra big wave hits the bows. *Joe would love this.* We've never come across in a storm before. But Joe isn't here. When I close my eyes, I can't even see his face.

'Is it all right?' A small child's voice keeps piping from the seat behind me. 'Is it safe? Are we going to drown?'

*   *   *

Five hours of it, sick bag on my lap, and I get my first glimpse of land. I've been watching for ages, rubbing a space in the misted-up window. *Land* starts as a faint shadow on the horizon, then another: low dark shapes floating on the water. My heart lifts. I love this moment. More and more shapes appear: clearly rocks now, not shadows, and at last the first proper islands. A cluster of white houses, small fields, an empty rain-swept beach. Almost there.

The ferry docks at Main Island. I'm on auto-pilot now, I've been travelling for so long. Queue to get off. Go along the harbour. Find the small ferries waiting to take passengers to the outer islands. The boat I want, the *Spirit,* is moored below stone steps, halfway along the harbour wall. Another queue.

I've got my hood up. It's still raining, though not as hard. I'm still feeling sick, like everyone else. I want to blend in with the crowd, be swept along, unrecognised. But the boat skipper, Dave, knows me instantly. He presses my hand as he helps me on to the boat.

10

'Freya! Good to have you back. OK? Bit of a wild crossing, I bet!'

I have to hold back tears. It hits me, suddenly, what it's going to be like. People knowing. Feeling sorry. Not knowing what to say. It's hard for everyone; I understand that, I really do. I know why people avoid it altogether, don't say anything rather than say the wrong thing. There isn't an easy way through any of this.

A fair-haired boy is doing the tickets. Not Huw, thank goodness. I make myself breathe properly: in, out, steady. People with rucksacks and tents and stuff pile into the boat. Jokes about the weather; camping. I let the voices wash over my head. Dave starts up the engine and the *Spirit* chugs slowly out of the sheltered harbour and across Broad Sound to St Ailla.

* * *

Evie is waiting on the jetty, waving wildly as the *Spirit* edges in. I wave back. I'm last off the boat. Dave and the boy start loading bags and camping stuff on to the tractor-trailer on the jetty, ready to take it to the campsite at Sally's farm and the holiday houses round the island. It was Huw's job, last summer.

The fair-haired boy turns to me. 'All right?' he says. 'Sling your bag on with the others and I'll bring it up to the house after I've done the campsite delivery.'

So he does know who I am.

Evie steps forward. 'Thanks, Matt,' she says. 'This is Freya, my granddaughter.'

Matt smiles. 'I guessed.'

11

He's got the bluest eyes.

Evie folds me in a big hug. Just for that moment I want to bury my head in the softness of her body and forget everything.

'Safe and sound, thank goodness,' Evie says. 'What a storm!' She hugs me even tighter. 'I'm so glad to see you, Freya. You can't imagine!'

The rain's almost stopped. I wait with Evie while Matt gets the tractor started up. We sit on the wall, watching the fog lifting off the water, while everyone else walks up the hill, turns off left to the pub or right to the campsite. Once everyone's disappeared, I let myself imagine we're the only people on the whole island.

The air's sweet after rain. Waves wash against the stone jetty. The tractor engine hums into the distance. For a moment, there's silence. Something drops away inside me. It's like an elastic band twanging free. I can breathe again. I'm here, at my favourite place on earth, where I can really be me.

But nothing is that simple any more. This is an island full of memories now. Full of ghosts, and secrets.

Three

Back at the house, I do what I always do when I get to Evie's, sort of check out each room for new things. I read the postcards that are propped along the mantelpiece in the sitting room. Evie and Gramps don't mind. It's like I'm catching up on what I've missed. Sometimes I think I've got two lives: the ordinary one, back home, and my one here, on the island. We've been coming here almost every summer since Evie and Gramps bought the house, seven years ago. That's half my life. I even have my own room.

The photographs are here just the same, of course, lined up along the bookcase: me, as a baby, at five and seven, eleven and thirteen, and the same for Joe, and one of Gramps in his funny white bee-keeper's suit, and lots of Dad, and the wedding one I love, because of the loving, happy way Dad's looking at Mum, and because I know their secret: that even though Mum looks slim and beautiful in her cream silk dress, baby Joe is there already, growing inside Mum, already five months big.

Now all the photos of Joe will stop. He'll be here, at sixteen, for ever, and never any older, while I'll go on growing up, and before long I'll be older and bigger than Joe and not his *little sister* any more . . .

I pick up the very last one of Joe. We didn't know that, of course, when Gramps took it. Joe's holding up three mackerel he's just caught, grinning into the camera. Behind him the sky is a brilliant blue.

'Tea?' Evie calls from the kitchen.

'Coming.'

The tractor rumbles up the lane from the farm. I hear the *thump* of my bag being dumped at the gate. Evie calls out, 'Thanks, Matt!'

Through the window I glimpse Matt's sun-bleached hair, the back of his blue T-shirt. The tractor chugs off again.

*   *   *

'Better phone home to say you're safe,' Evie says.

13

I nod. I don't want to talk to Mum right now. Don't really want to think about her, or Dad, or anything I've left behind back there, but Evie starts asking questions while we're drinking tea and waiting for Gramps to turn up. He's gone to fetch in the crab pots.

'It's good they let you come,' Evie says. 'That's progress, isn't it?'

'Yes.'

'How's your mum doing, now?'

'Same. She still can't work. But she's got the move and the house to sort out, so she's busy enough.'

'And Dad?'

'Still working all the time. He says he has to, because Mum's not earning anything. They argue about it.'

Evie's face closes up. I wish I hadn't said anything. I don't usually. Not even to Miranda. No one knows about all the arguments. Or the silences. The silences are the worst. I imagine too much. I'm scared it's all falling apart—them, our family . . .

Evie pulls herself together. 'Well, it's been such a tough year for you all. I'm so glad you're here, Freya. You're very pale. You look like you could do with a holiday.' She's got tears in her eyes.

I look away.

'We'll do our best. I know it's not much fun with just Gramps and me. But there are lots of kids at the campsite for you to play with; Sally says they're fully booked all August. Loads of families.' She smiles at me. 'Unless of course you're too grown-up to play this year, Freya May?'

'I wouldn't play anywhere else,' I say. 'But here,

14

it's different. Everything is.'

'Well!' Evie says. 'Thank heavens for that, at least. But it won't be easy, Freya. Everything will remind you of last year . . . bring it all back. You need to be prepared for that, yes?'

Of course I know that. But right now I can't speak, my throat too tight, choked with tears.

I want to tell Evie how much I love being in this house with her and Gramps, even though they're old and don't have a computer or anything much. Or perhaps *because* it's like that. Life is simple and easy. *Used* to be, anyway. But I don't tell her.

I lug my bag upstairs, trying to keep my mind off that boy—Matt—because it seems sort of disloyal, to be thinking about anyone but Joe. Silly, really. And it doesn't stop me, in any case. Matt's got fair hair like Huw, but he's younger, I guess. Eighteen, rather than twenty. I wonder what he knows about me, and Joe, and last summer. Is it all round the campsite? It was in all the newspapers at the time, of course. Accident. Inquest. Verdict. Sally might have told him.

Through the little bedroom window under the eaves I can see straight across fields to the sea, right out to the Bird islands, Annot and Kila, and the jagged shapes of the Western Rocks. *Don't think about that now*. I take a deep breath. I sit on the bed, run my fingers over the faded pink bedspread, the tiny neat stitches of the patchwork. When I was little, Evie used to tell me stories about the different scraps of material: bits of her mother's dresses, a patch of curtain.

The sky is beginning to clear.

I leave my bag untouched, go back down to the kitchen.

15

'I'm going out,' I tell Evie.

She nods. 'Look out for Gramps, then.'

*　　　*　　　*

The wind's blowing hard. I twist my hair into a rope and tuck it inside my collar. I'm going to do what Joe and I always do together, when we first arrive: walk right round the island. It's not far; only takes about an hour. I start by going through the cow field to the cliff, where there are huge rocks you can climb up.

Wherever you are, you can hear the sea, like a rhythm, a pattern of sound in your skull. Over time, it becomes so familiar you hardly notice it, but when you first arrive it hits you all over again. Today, because of the storm, the sea's still churned up, thundering and sucking and swooshing on to the rocks. The wind carries sea-spray—spindrift—which coats my hair and clothes in a fine mist. The sea has a voice. Today it's angry and wild. I love it. The wind whips my hair out from my collar as I begin to climb higher. It lashes thin wet strands across my face and makes it sting. It's like it's waking me up.

From the top, I can see almost the entire island, east to west. I stretch out my arms wide and lean into the wind. I gulp the sweet cold air, great lungfuls of it. I yell out, and the wind snatches my voice. The roar of the waves drowns it.

A thin streak of sunshine gleams on the sea over at Periglis. Gramps might be back with the crab pots by now. I climb down from my boulder perch and start making my way along the foreshore, skirting the bottom of the farm and the lower

16

fringes of the campsite, towards Periglis beach.

Voices.

Someone laughs.

Two people are sitting close together on the stone field boundary at the shore edge. One's a girl I don't recognise, with golden, wind-swept hair, in a big turquoise jumper and baggy orange trousers, bare feet. Looking at her intently, laughing, is the fair-haired boy from the boat. Matt.

My heart sinks. They've seen me. I'm not ready for this.

'Hello there!' The girl grins.

'Got your bag OK?' Matt asks.

I nod. Can't speak. My face is burning. I hurry on past, slipping on the wet seaweed and rocks. I know they're watching me. Wondering why I'm so rude. Or shy, or stupid. But when I glance back, I see they're holding hands, looking at each other. They've forgotten all about me already.

There's no sign of Gramps at the beach, but the rowing boat is stowed safely at the edge of the old lifeboat slipway. I try not to see the space where the dinghy used to be. Instead of going on round the island, I cut back to the lane. I can do the rest another time. The lane takes me past the empty house attached to the old lighthouse. The gate's hanging off its hinges, and one of the windows upstairs is broken. Nettles grow waist-high in the big front garden.

Something looks different. There's a notice pinned to a post in the garden: *For Sale*.

I'm dragging my feet.

Remembering.

Last summer.

Four

Last summer

We're sitting in the overgrown garden next to the old lighthouse, our backs against the sun-warmed wall. Joe's eyes are closed, his face lifted to the sun. He's so brown! He's been off school since his exams finished in June, and even before that he was on study leave, revising in the garden (not!) and getting a tan.

I study his face. He doesn't look so much like my brother these days. There's a line of dark stubble along his cheek and under his chin. He leaves a razor in the shower. He spends hours in the bathroom, door locked. He shuts his bedroom door.

He's stripped off his T-shirt. His chest is all muscly and his stomach is flat as a board. Dad teases him about the six-pack. Dad's jealous: when he sucks in his stomach it still sticks out and Mum laughs, but in a nice way. Joe works hard at being fit. Sometimes I go into the living room and he's on the floor doing press-ups and stomach crunches, red in the face like he's about to explode. Since we came here for the summer, Joe's been running almost every morning before I'm even up. I seem to be sleeping longer and longer. Evie say it's my age. I'm growing fast.

Not as fast as Joe, though. He's taller than

Gramps, and changing all the time. This is the first year he hasn't wanted me tagging along. He's worse at home: he won't even walk to town with me any more, in case he meets someone he knows. But here, because all the kids—all ages—play out on the field in the evenings, Joe can't stop me joining in. The first couple of weeks this summer he let me go fishing with him too, as long as I was quiet. He even showed me how to cast a line and we made spinners together. But lately that's changed. Joe's changed. He's not mean, exactly, just different to how he was before. And sometimes he's still lovely, the person I love best in the whole world. Miranda can't believe I feel like that. She and her brother squabble all the time.

'What are you looking at?' Joe growls, one eye open and squinting at me.

'Nothing.'

He stretches his legs out. They're all tanned and hairy. The sun has bleached the hairs. He closes his eyes again.

We've trampled down the weeds to make a place big enough to sit, hidden from the lane. It smells rank: hot roots, crushed stems and leaves. The pink flowers stink something rotten when you squash them. We stopped off here on our way back from the shop because Joe wanted to explore the garden: he's always on the lookout for old junk and stuff other people have thrown away. I just followed and he didn't say I couldn't.

'Why doesn't someone buy this place?' I say. 'Imagine living in the lighthouse! You

19

could have your bed at the top. All the furniture would have to be round.' We often think about different places to live. Joe wanted a tree house, for ages: not a play house but a real one, big enough to live in. 'This could be a lovely garden. There are roses and fruit trees and everything.'

'The house is a wreck,' Joe says. 'You'd have to spend a fortune doing it up. Bringing everything over by boat. It's not worth it.'

He gets up and I follow him. We beat a path through nettles and long grass to one of the windows and peer in. Hard to see through the dirty glass: I can just make out wooden floorboards, a fireplace, some sort of cupboard against the end wall.

Joe pulls at the window. Part of the wooden frame comes away in his hand. He laughs. 'See? The wood's all rotten. It'd be easy to get in.' He starts edging along to the door.

'Don't,' I say, suddenly uneasy. 'We shouldn't be here. It's private property.'

'No one's been here for years,' Joe says. 'Who's to know?' But he walks away from the house, back to our warm spot against the wall.

*   *   *

I pick off dead flowerheads from the rose that sprawls through a crab-apple tree. Joe looks like he's asleep. Next year he wants to do a boat-building course, instead of A levels, and leave home. He talks about crewing yachts round the world. He wants to travel, have adventures. He's full of plans and dreams. He tells me these things, but not Mum or Dad. They won't be happy about the no-A levels plan. Dad thinks Joe should be an architect, like him. I try to imagine home without Joe. My last birthday, he made me a cake with icing and everything. Not many brothers would do that.

'Will we swim, then?' I say, eventually. 'It's warm enough now. We can dump the shopping and then go to Beady Pool. Or the sand bar.'

'If the tide's low enough,' Joe says. We both know it's dangerous to swim there at high tide.

Joe doesn't move. Time stretches out. We might have been here for hours. The garden's hot and dusty. It hasn't rained for days, which is unusual, here. Even in high summer there are storms.

I'm desperate to go to the beach now. 'Come on, then,' I say.

Joe stretches his arms above his head, hands interlocked. His fingers crack. He yawns like a sleepy cat, and gets up.

'I'm going sailing this afternoon,' Joe says. 'I just remembered. Sorry, Freya.'

Five

Gramps taught Joe to sail when he was about nine. He tried to teach me too, but I didn't like it much. Joe loved it from the very beginning. The first time they went out, it got windy suddenly, and Joe just laughed. I see all the dangers. When I'm scared, I can't think. Sailing, I was scared most of the time, even on a calm day. But swimming is different. Swimming, I feel in control. I swim like a fish, strong and steady. Crawl and backstroke, butterfly and breaststroke. I like diving, swimming underwater, seeing how long I can hold my breath.

'Hey! Freya!'

Gramps is at the gate. I run the last bit of the lane and give him a big hug. He smells fishy, salty. He holds me tight for ages.

I wriggle free. 'The lighthouse is for sale,' I say, as if he doesn't know already.

'Some fool will be buying it for a holiday place, doing it up.' Gramps sniffs. 'They'll get more than they bargained for.'

I follow him through the front garden and round the side of the house to the back door. He points out the flowers he loves: he knows them all by name, as if they are children: *Alchemilla mollis*; *Verbena*; *Astrantia*; *Digitalis*. Foxglove. A bumblebee pushes up inside the purple bell-shaped flower. We used to put the flowers on our fingers like little hats, until Evie told us the flowers are poisonous.

Evie's washing her hands in the kitchen sink. 'You found each other, then.' She picks up the towel from the hook on the door. 'Supper's in about half an hour.'

Gramps grins. 'Time for a quick drink.' He pours beer for himself, and wine for Evie.

I go upstairs to unpack. I pause outside the room where Joe sleeps—slept. The door's ajar. I push it open, make myself go right in. The bed is made up, the dark blue bedspread smoothed over. Joe's pictures are still on the walls: the wrecks map, photographs of the Wayfarer dinghy, with Joe and Gramps standing next to it, a ten-year-old Joe in his wetsuit and Gramps looking more upright and smiley than he does now. There are framed drawings Joe did when he was younger: designs and plans of boats and buildings, mostly, drawn in fine black draughtsman's pen. I go over to the window and pick up the shells and stones and bleached bird skulls lined up neatly along the shelf. There's a pile of driftwood, some brass nails, and an old rusty winch he found on the beach.

There's no dust on anything. I imagine Evie in here, polishing the pebbles in her hands, dusting the sea-urchins and the dried-up starfish. I lift one of the sea-urchins; it is light and hollow in the palm of my hand. Joe's books—mostly secondhand, borrowed from Gramps or picked up in charity shops—are neatly stacked along the other shelf. *The Kon-Tiki Expedition*; *Mountains of the Mind*; *The Perfect Storm*; *Spear Fishing for Beginners*. Joe wasn't your average sixteen-year-old. He wasn't like anyone else I've ever known.

But that's the before Joe.

Joe before Sam arrived and changed him.

*   *   *

'Fancy a quick walk?' Evie says, after supper. 'I need to see Sally, at the farm. Then we could go along the shore to the pub.'

'What happened to the puppies? Did Sally find homes for them?' I ask.

'All bar one,' Evie says. 'She kept the one you loved, after all. You can come with me and see her, if you like.'

Gramps and I wait in the yard while Evie talks to Sally. Gramps wanders into the greenhouse where Sally grows vegetables to sell to the campsite people. Leggy tomato plants scrabble for light among courgettes and peppers. Gramps tuts at the weeds. His own greenhouse is immaculate.

Two dogs come bounding out of the kitchen. One's Bonnie, the mother dog; she wags her tail and comes to sit right close up on my feet, a warm weight against me, so I can fondle her silky ears. The other one barks and dances. She doesn't look anything like the small, cuddly puppy from last year. She doesn't remember me.

'What's her name?'

Gramps shakes his head. He's hopeless at remembering things like that.

Evie and Sally come to the door.

'Hello, Freya. Lovely to see you! You've found Bess, then.'

Last summer, I wanted her so badly I could cry. I've wanted a dog for as long as I can remember. Mum always says no. In my head, the puppy was called Tilly. Now I've got to get used to calling her Bess.

'She's grown so big!' I say.

'She's a bundle of energy,' Sally says. 'Any time

you want, take her out with you.'

The dogs have the run of the place. They don't need to be taken for walks because they can go wherever they want, more or less. So Sally is just being kind.

Bonnie trots behind us as we make our way down the track to the gate and the camping field.

'Bess!' I call.

She runs, barks, and rushes back to the farmhouse.

'Never mind,' Evie says. She knows I'm disappointed.

*   *   *

The campsite's full of brightly coloured tents packed close together in the honeycomb of tiny stone-hedged fields that run between the farmhouse and the shoreline. People are queuing with pots and pans for space at the sinks outside the stone barn. Evie and Gramps keep stopping to chat, so I go on ahead.

'We'll meet you at the bench above Periglis,' Evie calls after me.

*   *   *

I'm concentrating on my feet, stepping from one slippery rock to the next along the tideline, when something makes me glance up. Two small girls are digging in the sand further down, quite close to the water. Beyond them, out on the long, thin promontory of stones that's revealed at low tide, is Joe. I stop dead. It's him, Joe, in his usual black T-shirt and dark blue jeans, standing at the very

25

end, casting a line into the deep water. His box of fishing stuff is balanced on the stones at his feet. He's sideways on, his messy brown hair blowing over his face so I can't see it, but I don't need to. I know it is Joe. My hands are clammy with sweat, my heart hammering against my ribcage. He's so solid and real, so not a ghost. It doesn't make sense, but there he is. I can see him plain as anything.

I start running towards him, sliding and slipping. The girls look up as I run past. One is Rosie, from last year. She stands up, ready to speak to me but I don't stop. Water splashes up my leg as I skid in a shallow pool. I'm holding my breath again. Any moment I'm expecting him to go. *Stay there!* I will him. *Wait for me!*

I call out, but he doesn't seem to hear. 'Joe!'

Nearly there.

'Joe!'

He turns.

*   *   *

It isn't him.

It's a boy like Joe, a younger version, with the same sort of clothes and messy hair, but a different face.

Blood rushes into mine. *Stupid.*

I'm still standing there, like a lemon, when he says something. His voice is young, light—so unlike Joe's I almost laugh.

'All right?' he says.

I nod. 'Sorry. Thought you were someone . . .'

I start scrabbling back over the rocks, slipping and stumbling. I stub my toe. I grit my teeth so I won't cry.

'Freya!' Rosie's high voice calls after me as I run past. I want to hide, just long enough to pull myself together, but there's nowhere on the beach, so I scuff along the top to the bench near the footpath and sit down. I wait there, heart pounding, fists tight. Every so often I glance at the boy, fishing. Easy enough to make a mistake. From a distance. In the fading light.

Gramps and Evie make their way slowly along the footpath. They come to sit one each side of me. We don't speak. Squashed in the middle, I start to feel calmer again. I shut my eyes till I can't see Joe's face any more and my heart's stopped thumping so bad. There's a pain there that won't go away, though. Ever.

'Look at that!' Evie says eventually.

The sky's amazing. Pink and gold in stripes nearest the horizon, fading through turquoise to pale blue mottled with silver cloud like the skin of a mackerel. The red-gold disc of sun slips into the water as we watch.

'Let's go and get a drink at the pub,' Gramps says.

We cross the field, navigating the football game which I know will play on long after it's too dark to see. It's the same every summer. Rosie and her friend are playing along the edge, and Matt and the girl with the braided hair are running, laughing, after the ball. I think I see the fishing boy, at the far end of the pitch, still too much like Joe.

'Do you want to join in?' Evie asks. 'We can come back for you later, if you like?'

I shake my head, even though the voices tug at

me. We go on past the church. Echoes of shouts, laughter, follow us on the breeze. Evie links her arm with mine as we go along the darkening lane. Now, ahead, the pub shines out like a beacon.

We step over the threshold into the bright light. A crowd of people are pushing to get to the bar, ordering drinks and meals. A boat trip from Main Island must have just landed. Gramps tuts and joins the queue, and Evie and I go back outside to find a table. It's completely dark now. I'm tired out. Voices merge, drift, wash over my head.

Going back afterwards is like sleepwalking. The field's empty. A layer of mist skims the surface of the grass, lit up for an instant by the beam of the lighthouse as it swings round. The sea churns stones, speaks a language just out of my reach. Back home, in bed, I can still hear it. It sighs, whispers. Just as I'm dropping off, Joe's deep voice breathes into my ear. *Freya?*

Six

**Last summer
August 12th**

It's raining. Evie's gone shopping on Main Island and Gramps has disappeared off somewhere too. Joe's making floats. He cuts off a small chunk of wood, carves it into a rough oval with a penknife and sandpapers it until it's completely smooth. He drills a hole at either end, makes two wire loops and glues them in. He fixes a swivel hook at one end and a treble hook at the other. He paints the fish shape with silver and blue like a tiny mackerel. He gives it an eye of epoxy resin. Last of all he varnishes it. Every step, he takes his time. His hand with the fine paintbrush is steady and meticulous. He lines up the fish floats on a sheet of newspaper on the kitchen table.

'Can I do one?'

Joe pauses mid-brushstroke; he looks at me, amused. 'How bored are you, Freya?'

'On a scale of one to ten, ten.'

Joe goes back to concentrating on getting the markings right.

'How do you remember?' I ask.

He shrugs. 'Seen enough mackerel,' he says.

He has an almost photographic memory for some things. When he wants, that is. I can imagine him building boats. Beautiful wooden ones, that cost thousands of pounds. Mum says he's been like this—clever at making things—since he was really little.

He hands me a chunk of wood. I pick up the penknife and start whittling the shape. Slivers of wood curl off the knife and drop on to the table.

'Hold the knife so you're cutting away from your hand,' Joe says.

I don't do too badly. Once I'm sandpapering, it's almost the right shape. Joe does the wire bits for me, and the glue. Painting is more fun. I copy one of Joe's, to get the pattern right. Only my brush must be bigger or something, because the lines are a bit thick and fuzzy. I lay it next to Joe's.

'It's not as good.'

'It's fine,' Joe says. 'The fish won't mind, anyway.'

I fidget about for a while longer. Joe makes me wash the brushes. I stare out over the wet garden. The rain's stopped. 'Shall we go and see the puppies at the farm?' I say to Joe.

'You can.'

'Do you think they'll let us have one?'

'Who?'

'Mum and Dad.'

'No.'

'Will you say you really, really want one too? Please?'

Joe sighs. 'But I don't.'

'You used to.'

'That was ages ago. I won't even be at home after next year. There's no point.'

*   *   *

Sally's made a special pen for the puppies in the scullery just off the farm kitchen. The mother dog, Bonnie, can easily jump over the side but it keeps the puppies safe. They're heaped together in one corner, half asleep, a squirming pile of puppies. 'Help yourself,' Sally says. She's sorting piles of papers at the table.

Bonnie comes wagging over. She knows me well, so she doesn't mind me stroking her puppies. They are Border collies: black and white and very furry. My favourite is the smallest female, with a black face and hardly any white patches. I play over this scene in my mind: when Mum and Dad arrive at the end of August they see me and the puppy together and they say, 'Well, you're obviously made for each other,' and we take her back with us. My own puppy like I've wanted ever since I was about five.

I'll do all the looking after—the walks and food and grooming and everything. I'll call her Tilly. I'll train her properly because Border collies are really intelligent and need to be busy, learning stuff. Bonnie is a working dog on Sally's farm. Our garden at home is a bit small, but there's a wall round it so at least it's safe, and there's the canal towpath really nearby for walks. She can round up the ducks.

I pick up my puppy and she squeaks. She's so warm. I bend my head over her and she licks my face with her rough pink tongue and wags her tail which makes her bottom wiggle too. Puppies can leave their mother when they're eight or nine weeks, which is about perfect timing for the end of August when we'll go back home at the end of the summer holidays.

Bonnie jumps up to check her puppy's OK. She's such a good mother. Tilly gets so excited and wriggly I nearly drop her so I put her down quick. 'There you go, Tilly-Little.'

The puppy pushes up against Bonnie who flops over so she can feed. All the puppies plough in for a share. They paddle with their paws to make the milk come. Bonnie lets out a huge sigh.

'She's had enough. We need to start weaning the pups soon,' Sally says. 'And find them homes.'

$$*\qquad*\qquad*$$

Evie's unpacking a huge box of groceries when I get back. There's no sign of Joe or the fishing floats.

'Wouldn't you like one of the farm puppies?' I ask her.

'I've got enough to be looking after already,' she says. 'With your gramps!'

'I'd do all the looking after her when I was here,' I say. 'Every summer.'

'For how much longer, though?' Evie says. 'You won't want to be coming here for ever, Freya. You're growing up.'

'I'll never stop coming here,' I say. 'It's my favourite place anywhere in the whole world.'

Evie makes a sound, a sort of *hmmm*. 'The world's a big place,' she says. 'And it's all just waiting for you and Joe. You'll see.'

Seven

My third morning, this summer. Evie sends me up to the farm to get some milk and stuff. I have to queue with the campsite people at the back door. I read the notices chalked up on the blackboard: *Fresh farm veg: courgettes and tomatoes. Organic lamb burgers; organic minced beef. Milk, cream, yoghurt. Boat trip to seals 7pm. Shower tokens 20p.*

32

'Hi.' The girl with the hair, Matt's friend, leans against the door frame. Sky-blue cotton trousers and a green top today. She's got an amazing tan, and three silver belly button rings.

'I keep seeing you,' she says. 'You're Evie's granddaughter?'

I nod.

'Izzy. Dairymaid,' she introduces herself. She speaks with a local accent, but I've never seen her other years. 'Also campsite cleaner, events organiser, occasional boat hand and general dogsbody.' She laughs, looks at me all wide-eyed.

I suddenly realise she's waiting for me to say something. 'Freya,' I say.

'Glad to meet you, Freya.' She has an odd way of talking. Sort of old-fashioned polite but as if she's laughing, too. 'How may I help you?'

'Milk. Two pints. One pot of natural yoghurt. Please.'

'Hang on, then.' She goes to fetch the stuff from the big fridges in the barn.

While I'm waiting I look into the kitchen and out through its window to the back garden, where Tilly/Bess is playing with a ball. I'm just thinking about calling her over when footsteps thump down the stairs and Matt appears. He stuffs his feet into old wellies by the door. He grins at me. 'Coming on the boat trip this evening?'

I'm suddenly tongue-tied.

'You should. See the seals,' Matt says.

Izzy reappears. 'Yes. It'll be fun. Seven o'clock at the jetty. See you there?' She hands me the milk and the yoghurt. 'Yes?'

I can't work out whether they're being extra nice on purpose, because of what they've heard about

33

me, or because it's Izzy's job, or what. Perhaps that's just how she is. She has this open, smiling face and all that golden hair and she's sort of brimming over with something. Happiness? Confidence? I notice it because it's the opposite of me, right now. And because it's a shock to realise that. *This* me isn't the one I used to be.

I think about that when I'm lying in the garden later. I can't read. I start, but my mind drifts off and away and I lose track. I doodle with a pen in my notebook with the blue cover, but I don't write, either. I draw a maze pattern, like the one on the cliff. Next I sketch a shape that becomes a sea-urchin shell. I shade in the stripes. It's like I need to pin things down on the paper. Everything might just as easily float off, like thistledown. I have to make myself stay there, seeing and hearing the world around me. I try to draw the foxgloves, and a bee. I draw the tiny yellow pollen bags on its legs. I draw another shape, like a fish.

I get up, legs stiff from being still too long. The shed door creaks when I push it and spiders scuttle into the corner as sunlight trickles in through the open doorway. I find Joe's box on the shelf, a year of dust settled on the lid. It stains my fingers. Inside, everything's still perfectly organised, exactly how Joe left it last summer. Hooks and spinners, flies, a ball of fine line, a series of floats in the neat compartments. There are three perfect hand-painted mackerel floats, and the messy one I made. He kept it, then.

I try to imagine Joe now, standing behind me and leaning over my shoulder to see into the tackle box. I try to feel his breath against the back of my neck.

Nothing.

How long have I been standing here?

Evie peers round at me. 'Saw the shed door was open,' she says. 'You'll find the rods at the back, if you're thinking of going fishing.'

I'm not. At least, I hadn't been planning that at all. But why not? If Joe's anywhere on this island, he's most likely to be out on the fishing rock below Wind Down. That's where he'll come to me, if he's going to.

I don't exactly think this out, not as clearly as this, because if I did I'd see how really mad it sounds. It's more a feeling, pushing me to do things I wouldn't normally. I don't really like fishing much. It's Joe's thing, for starters, and you have to stay still and quiet for ages, just hanging around, and then if you do catch anything it's all rather horrible: the hook stuck in flesh, and the goggling eyes, and the flapping about and everything. Seeing a fish in air is like how I imagine drowning, for a person. Gasping for breath.

That's three good reasons not to do it, but here I am, already brushing cobwebs and dust off the two fishing rods. I try winding the reels. One's rusted up. I take the other one outside into the garden, and the box. I haven't much of a clue how to do it, since I've never done it by myself before, but I reckon I can always ask someone. That boy, even.

Or Matt.

Why do I keep thinking about him?

I'm feeling braver today, so I risk going the quick way via the campsite to get to Wind Down. There aren't many people around as it's nearly midday and quite sunny, so people are at the beach

35

already or off on boats or whatever. There's no sign of anyone I know from other years. Nor the boy.

Outside a big, hexagonal orange tent someone's propped a board pinned with home-made jewellery against a camping chair. I stop to look. The earrings, necklaces and bracelets are made from bits of shell and pebble and tiny feathers strung on silver wire.

The tent door unzips. Izzy pokes her head out. 'Hi, Freya!'

'Hi!' I know I'm blushing. Stupid. Again.

'Like them?' Izzy asks.

I nod. 'Are they yours? You made them?'

'Yep. Necklaces seven pounds. Earrings two pounds fifty. Real silver. Bargains.'

'They're lovely,' I say. They really are. The colours, the delicate designs.

'Thanks,' Izzy says.

There's an awkward moment: her half in, half out of the tent, me standing there.

'Is this where you're living?' I ask.

'Yes. Third tent since April. Two got ripped, in storms, but this one's extra good. It's my mum's.'

'Since *April*? In a *tent*?'

Izzy laughs. 'Mad, yes? I came over soon as we got study leave for A levels. My mum went mental! I went back to do the actual exams. Then I got the summer job here. But this tent's properly waterproof and really cosy inside. See?' Izzy holds open the flap so I can see inside.

And it is amazing. Like a Bedouin tent or a yurt or something exotic like that: Indian bedspreads and rugs and cushions, everything bathed in a pinky-gold light from the sun filtering through the

36

fabric.

A head sticks up from under an orange blanket and stares, bleary-eyed, at Izzy and me. It's Matt.

'What's the time?' he mumbles.

'Twelve? One? Time you got up,' Izzy says.

For a second I'm confused. Haven't I already seen Matt, up at the farmhouse, earlier this morning? He must have to get up early for milking, and the first boat . . . So maybe that's why he's gone back to bed. And then I see the look he gives Izzy, and I go hot all over. Duh! Izzy and Matt haven't been just sleeping . . .

I duck back out of the tent. Izzy whispers something to Matt, and he laughs. There's the soft thud of someone lying down, and I don't stay to hear anything more. I know they're not laughing at me. I know that. They won't give me another thought. I start to run, the rod and the box banging against my legs. All the way, I keep thinking of Mum and Dad, the way they used to be. Izzy, in her bright, silly clothes with that big happy smile. Matt's soft mouth, finding hers.

I want to cry. I don't though. I've stopped doing that all the time. It cured me, hearing Mum night after night. It doesn't do any good, not after a while.

I decide I'll just go and sit on the fishing rocks; I don't have to fish, I'll just see what it's like sitting there. And I can think about Joe, and see what happens. If no one else is there, that is.

But someone is. Why am I surprised, even, that it's that boy again? Joe's shadow. I'm about to turn back but he's seen me and he waves. So I go on. He stands up, and he walks to the edge of the biggest rock which is nearest the cliff, and he holds his hand out to help me do the jump across the gap, as if he knows I might be scared, but without saying anything. So I start liking him a bit, right then.

I've done the jump across before. It's better not to look down. It's hardly any distance across, but there's a deep drop and the sea is always boiling and churning as it's squeezed along the gap between the rocks. If you fell you'd be smashed up quite badly.

'It's a good place for mackerel,' the boy says. 'They come in really close, because the water's so deep.'

'I know,' I say. 'I've been here loads of times.'

He threads a silver sand eel on to a hook. Casts the line out. Stands with his back to me. I wait. It's so like being with Joe I can hardly breathe. My hands shake when I try to open the box.

'It's my first holiday here,' the boy says. 'Every one else at the campsite seems to have been a million times. Are you camping?'

'No.'

'Nice fishing rod,' he says after a long gap.

I almost laugh, but I can see how shy he is, and he's trying to be friendly, and Miranda's a long way away and she'll never know about this particular conversation, so I make a big effort to be friendly back.

'It was my grandpa's,' I say. 'I stay with him and my gran every summer. I'm Freya.'

'Danny,' he says. 'You can borrow some bait, if you want.'

For one horrible moment I think he's about to hand me a heap of pink wriggling meal worms. But he shoves a bucket with his foot. 'Help yourself.'

And that's how I come to hook my first ever sand eel, eyes wide open, holding my breath. *Sorry*, I say in my head to the sand eel as I skewer it. I catch my first ever mackerel by myself soon after. Me and Danny catch three each. After the first one, Danny takes over the actual killing bit, flipping the fish against the rock so it dies quickly, but I'm glad I've done one, at least. Joe would be proud of me. I can almost hear his voice, telling me. But he's not here. There's no sense of him at the fishing rock today, and I know there can't be, not with Danny here too.

Danny's excitement is catching. He does a kind of dance there on the rock. He'd go on catching fish after fish, if he had his way.

'That's enough,' I tell him. 'We shouldn't be greedy. Just get enough for supper.'

We walk back together. Danny's already planning a barbecue. He's seen too many of those telly programmes—cooking wild food . . . living off the land . . . whatever. He talks about finding edible seaweed and all sorts. 'We might find marsh samphire, if we look. It tastes a bit like asparagus.'

He sees my face. 'What is it? What's the matter? Freya?'

'Got to go.' I manage to spit out the words. Then I start running.

I leave him way behind, looking puzzled, those stupid dead fish dangling from his line. I don't care what Danny thinks any more. All I can think about is getting away, being alone. *Samphire*. The name no one's said for nearly a year.

Eight

Last summer
August 14th

Dave and Huw take the *Spirit* over to Main Island to pick up people from the ferry two or three times a week, to bring them back to the campsite on St Ailla. If the weather's good enough, all of us kids go down to the jetty to meet the boat and see who's arriving. We sit on the wall and watch the *Spirit* ploughing back across the Sound, and we help with loading the bags and gear on to the tractor-trailer. Sometimes, if Huw's driving he'll give us a lift back. Everyone loves the bumpy ride along the track to the field.

So that's what we're doing now: waiting. Me, Joe, Will, Luke, Lisa, Maddie, Rosie. Rosie is the youngest (about six) then me (thirteen). Maddie, Rosie's big sister, is the next oldest, then Joe, Will, Luke and Lisa are all sixteen. Huw's more like nineteen, and Dave's grown-up of course, like forty or even more.

'Where's Ben?' Rosie asks.

Maddie shrugs. 'Off somewhere.'

Ben lives on St Ailla all year round. He loves it when we all turn up in the summer: it means he gets to play football. He's not very good at it because he never gets any practice. He's about eleven or twelve. Small for his age. He goes to school by boat, on Main Island.

How cool is that?

'He said he was going to Main Island on the early boat with his dad,' Lisa says. 'That family with twin babies left this morning, too.'

'The campsite's full now, apparently,' Will says. 'Just one new family, arriving on the ferry.'

'I hope there's a girl for me to play with,' Rosie says.

'Me too. So you stop bothering us all the time,' Maddie says.

Rosie puckers up her mouth and slaps Maddie's leg. Maddie picks up a pebble and pretends she's going to hit Rosie, just so Rosie squawks, then chucks it at the can we've set up on a rock. She misses.

I have a go. I miss too.

Joe picks up a handful of pebbles. He chooses them carefully, testing their weight. He aims. The can bounces off the rock and clatters down the cliff a little way. 'Yes!' Joe jumps down from the wall and goes to set the can up again.

'Best of three,' Will says.

'Boat's coming,' Lisa calls.

We watch the people getting off. A few rambler types, for the bed and breakfast place, we guess. The family with camping gear is just a woman and two girls, one about seven, so Rosie's happy, and the other older, more like Joe's age. She's got long straight dark hair, almond eyes. She's utterly beautiful. A sort of collective sigh passes from Will to Luke to Joe and even to Lisa and

Maddie.

Huw helps the girl up the steps. He holds her arm longer than is strictly necessary. We all notice.

When I look round at Joe, I see his mouth's slightly open. 'Catching flies, fish-face?' I tease, and he shoves me so I fall off the wall.

The new girl doesn't smile. We watch her follow the woman and the little girl up the steep stone jetty. No one else moves or says anything. It's like we're all spellbound. As she goes past, she glances briefly at us. Rosie hops down and runs after the little girl. 'Hello, my name is Rosie.' We hear her chattering after them, like she always does with new people. The rest of us turn our heads to watch their progress along the path. The girl stops and looks back once. Joe smiles. Then Huw comes chugging past on the tractor, and we all scramble to get a lift with the luggage on the trailer. I see Joe check the labels on the bags.

That's the real moment Joe's summer changes. The day Samphire arrives.

Nine

'I thought I'd go on the boat trip tonight,' I say at teatime. Evie and I have grilled the mackerel and we're eating it now, picking out the small bones.

Evie shoots a look at Gramps, and then at me. 'Well,' she says slowly. 'I'm not sure . . . your mum and dad might not think that's a good idea . . .'

'Please?' I say. I know *why* they fret about me going on boats. Even so.

'I suppose we could come too,' Evie says.

Gramps snorts. 'Whatever for? I've seen enough seals to last a lifetime.'

'It's not just about the seals,' Evie says. 'It'll be fun.'

'It's OK,' I say. 'I'll be perfectly safe. Please. I want to go by myself. I'm fourteen, you know. Not a baby.'

I can see her wavering, trying to decide.

'All right. But be very careful. Hold on tight. And take my waterproofs,' she says. 'You'll need them.'

*   *   *

She's right. Out of the shelter of the islands the sea's still rough and churned up from the big storm. The waves seem huge, the boat suddenly tiny. But everyone's just laughing as waves break and spray drenches the deck. People start singing. It *is* fun, once I stop thinking too much about how far out we are, how deep the water is beneath. And everyone's there: Izzy and Matt and Danny. Maddie and Lisa from last year come up and say hello and no one mentions Joe or last summer, thank goodness, because it's obviously not the right time, and somehow it all feels easier to handle today.

'I'm freezing!' Lisa crosses over to sit on the slatted bench behind the wheelhouse. Maddie joins her, huddled up in her quilted jacket, and Danny plonks himself down in the space next to me.

Matt and Izzy are leaning out at the front of the

43

boat, Izzy laughing as usual. Dave yells at them from the wheelhouse and Matt pulls her back. He kisses her. She closes her eyes. I can't look away. There's something magnetic, magical even, about them. *What does it feel like, being kissed like that?*

'There! See? Loads of seals!' a voice calls out, and everyone surges to one side. The boat rocks.

'Sit down! Keep her balanced,' Dave growls. 'You'll all get a look. Stop panicking.'

'They look almost human,' Danny says. 'Those eyes.'

'Whiskery humans,' I say.

Two come right close up, heads high above the waves. They're watching us watching them.

'These are grey Atlantic seals. Another month or so and they'll start giving birth . . .' Dave begins the usual patter. I've heard it loads of times, but I still love looking at the seals. I can imagine each seal is a person, treading water. I watch one dive, begin counting. I start to feel dizzy: I can't help holding my own breath, waiting for the seal to come back up. My lungs push against my ribs till they hurt.

'How do they stay under so long?' Danny says.

'Mammalian diving reflex,' I say. 'They store oxygen in their blood and muscles, instead of in the lungs like we do.'

Matt and Izzy listen too.

'But people have the same reflex, up to a point,' I tell Danny. 'Your body goes into oxygen-saving mode when your face goes under. Heart rate slows down and everything. You can practise holding your breath.'

Not for ten minutes, though. Not for half an hour, like seals. Not for long enough, if you're trapped underwater.

44

'She's clever, that Freya,' Izzy says to Matt. He kisses her again and this time I'm looking away, suddenly sick and cold to the bone.

'You're shivering,' Danny says.

A small girl squeezes in next to him. He puts his arm round her. His little sister. She's the little girl I saw before on the beach, playing with Rosie.

It begins to rain.

'Back to the pub?' Dave asks and a cheer goes up from the boat. He revs the engine and the boat begins to turn. Only Izzy and Matt stay at the front, oblivious to the rain and the spray, hands clasped together, yelling with each roll and tip of the boat as it rides the waves back to our island. They look like people in a film. Izzy's hair is plastered to her head, sodden, and yet she's still beautiful, radiant. Matt sees it, and so does everyone else.

'Camping in the rain again,' someone says. 'Oh joy.'

'It'll blow out by morning,' Dave says. 'Tomorrow will be fine.'

*   *   *

I don't go to the pub with everyone. I come straight home, peel off the waterproofs—which aren't—and the layers of wet clothes underneath and get warm in the bath. Rain's still battering the window when I'm lying in bed. I think about the tents in the field, the sound of rain drumming on nylon, the damp seeping up from the grass. I imagine Izzy and Matt curled round each other in their nest of duvet and blankets. I'm almost asleep, half dreaming.

45

Am I asleep? In my muddled dream-thoughts, Joe is outside in the wind and the rain. Not a spirit Joe, but a real flesh and blood Joe, cold and wet and alone. And it's my fault. Why don't I do something? I need to find someone to help. I need to call him back. I'm caught in a nightmare maze and every turning takes me further away from where I want to be. I'm hotter and hotter and something tight is winding round my chest, smothering me.

I wake with a start, my heart thrumming under my ribs. I'm bound tight by the twisted sheet. Outside, the wind is shrieking, pulling at the window latch, trying to get in. I untangle the sheet and sit up. It's just after midnight. I'm so thirsty. I make my way downstairs. The light's still on.

Evie's reading on the sofa. She looks up. 'Freya! You look hot! What's up?'

I ease myself next to her so she can feel my forehead. I'm shivering now, my feet freezing. She tucks me under the garden rug, next to her.

'I was dreaming,' I say. 'And the wind woke me.'

'It makes such a strange noise, sometimes,' Evie says. 'Like it's moaning. It sounds almost human, doesn't it? I was wide awake too. So I came back downstairs to read. I don't like to disturb your gramps. He's terrible if he doesn't get enough sleep.'

Evie strokes my hair back from my face. 'Perhaps you've got a temperature. You caught a chill, maybe, from the boat. I'll get you some water. You stay there.'

She gets me a drink, and makes tea for herself, and I listen to the sounds from the kitchen of the tap running, and the kettle going on, and her feet padding round on the tiles, the chink of the cup on the table. I start to feel safe again. It's like being very little, when someone else is looking after you and you don't have to think or do anything for yourself. It hasn't been like that for me for a long time.

When Evie comes back she tucks the blanket round me again. She sort of pats me, and we sit together in the circle of light from the lamp on the side table, and we don't say anything. Evie finishes her tea.

'You're missing Joe,' she says at last. 'Of course you are.'

I look at her. She's lost in her own thoughts. There are tears on her cheeks. It's a comfort, sitting together like that, without having to say anything.

I don't even remember going back up to bed, but I must have, because that's where I am, next thing, and it's the morning: bright sunlight is flooding through the window and my phone says 11.06.

Ten

'It's a swimming day!' I tell Evie in the kitchen.

'How are you, this morning?'

'Completely better.' I give Evie a hug. 'The sun makes everything seem OK.'

'Why don't we take a picnic, have a swim and go over to Gara? The three of us, together. Go and tell Gramps. He's in the garden.'

I find him up by the hives, at the far end of the garden, reciting lines from some poem to the bees.

47

He often does that. He says it calms them down.

' "*Time held me green and dying*
Though I sang in my chains like the sea." '

He stops when he sees me. 'Here she is. Young Fern.'

'Freya, not Fern. Who's Fern?'

'She's in the poem. Or the place is Fern. I get muddled up.'

Evie calls Gramps *muddle-head* sometimes, and he doesn't seem to mind. It's true, for one thing, and it doesn't matter because bees and gardens and crab pots don't mind a bit of a muddle. In any case, Evie's bright and quick enough for two, Gramps says. People who are a bit muddly sometimes are restful to be with, I think. You don't have to be on your guard or worry about what you say.

'Coming for a picnic?' I ask him.

'Delighted, Madame.' Gramps gives a mock bow. The bees start buzzing round his head and he puts his hat back on quick. He takes my arm as if he's escorting me somewhere exciting, not just back down the garden to the kitchen door. He used to mess around and play like that much more than he does these days.

*   *   *

The tide's low. It's perfect for swimming from the long stretch of sand we call the Bar, between St Ailla and the next tiny island called Gara. Gramps drinks coffee and reads the newspaper while Evie and I get undressed. I squeeze into my wetsuit.

'I've grown! Can you help do me up?'

Evie has to tug the zip up my back and it still

48

doesn't fasten at the top.

'You need a new one!'

We don't mention the wetsuit still hanging in the shed, gathering dust. The wetsuit that might have helped save Joe, had he been wearing it. What would it feel like, to put it on? Like slipping into my brother's skin? Stepping into his shoes . . .

'Hurry up!' Evie calls from the water. She's already in, floating on her back, toes up, arms sculling. I'm not half as brave as her. The first time, I have to inch in, little by little, getting used to the cold. After that it's fine.

We swim overarm, side by side, a long way out, then turn to look back at the beach. Gramps has the binoculars trained on us. We wave. I think of those words from another poem: *not waving but drowning.* Everything is conspiring to remind me of Joe. As if there's any chance of me ever forgetting! Only Joe didn't wave. Didn't look back once.

Evie and I float for a while, and then we practise diving for pebbles. For the first time, I'm so much better than her! I've been practising holding my breath in the bath for years.

She comes up spluttering. 'OK. You win! You're almost a mermaid, Freya!'

We swim slowly back to the sand bar, breaststroke. Evie's out of breath, but I'm still full of energy. I love that feeling. I could swim for miles.

Gramps is waiting, holding out two towels. He folds me in the big blue one and holds on to me just that bit longer than usual, to let me understand how he feels, watching us go that far out. Evie's like me: she loves swimming. She loves

49

to be in the water. Not Gramps, though. He likes to be *on* the water. In a boat, with a sail and a rudder and a painter and a map and compass. *Horses for courses*, he says. He finds it hard, the way we swim right out, because he knows about tides and currents and what happens when you get cold or cramp. Over the years, he's got used to Evie doing it.

He picks seaweed out of my hair while we sip coffee from the flask and eat the crab sandwiches. We walk the whole length of the sand bar to Gara, our feet sliding in the dry sand near the dunes at the top. We trek up the hill through bracken tall enough to hide in, as far as the heathery top near the standing stone. Gramps walks more slowly; I run ahead and lean against the rough stone to wait. Evie's holding Gramps' hand. She looks much younger than him. Funny how I've not noticed that before.

Evie flops down on the heather. She pulls Gramps down too. 'Try it, Freya! Like a springy mattress.'

It is. I close my eyes in the sun. My head's full of the buzzing of honeybees, and the sweet smell of the heather flowers.

'Are they your bees, Gramps?'

'Yes,' he says. 'Don't you recognise them?'

I open my eyes. He's grinning, teasing me.

'Of course,' I say. 'Those stripy vests they're wearing. I'd know them anywhere.'

When I sit up, Gramps and Evie are lying at an angle to each other. Evie rests her head on Gramps' broad chest. They're breathing deeply, rhythmically, as if they're asleep. I wander back up to the stone, and the cairn just a bit further along

50

the peaty path. I can see right over the island from here to Broad Sound beyond, the deep channel of water between here and Main Island. A small sailing dinghy's tacking up the middle, leaving a faint trail on the surface of the sea. I watch it make its way up the Sound and out into the open sea till it's just a white dot on the horizon. Sea and sky are almost the exact same blue. A faint line marks where sky meets water. The longer I look, the more they merge until it's impossible to say which is which. It could be Joe, sailing out like that, into the blue, if things had been different. And suddenly, clear as the sound of the bees in the purple heather, I hear Joe's voice.

'*It's all right now.*'

I spin round. No one's there. I look, and strain to listen. My heart's racing again. Wind blows through the low heather bushes. Further off, a gull squawks.

There's really no one there. I must have imagined it, conjured the voice up from thinking so much about him. Even so . . .

'Ready to go back, Freya?' Evie calls from below. 'Or you can stay a bit longer. Just keep an eye on the tide.'

I skid down the track to join them. 'It's OK. I'll come now, with you.'

We push back down the hill through the bracken. The roots give off a sweet earthy scent where our feet bruise them.

That voice—Joe—has unnerved me. I have the peculiar feeling of being on some edge, in danger of slipping away altogether. I need to do something—say something—just to anchor me back to earth.

51

'Isn't that old well somewhere near here?' I ask. 'The Bronze Age one.'

'It's much further along, nearer Beady Pool,' Evie says. 'We can have a look for it if you like. It's quite difficult to find among the long grass.'

Gramps used to tell us stories about the islanders long ago throwing gifts into the well—coins, jewellery—and making wishes. They'd wish for a ship to be sent on to the rocks, so they'd get all the pickings from the shipwreck. 'Gruesome lot,' Gramps would say. 'But that's island life for you. Needs must.'

We haven't been here for a long time. We find it eventually, hidden by long grass and bracken near the cliff above Beady Pool. It smells peaty and damp. The air's cold, as if the sun never reaches it.

'Careful,' Evie says. 'It's deep, you know.'

It's too dark to see anything. I shuffle forward and grip on to the stone lip so I can look right down.

'Please don't,' Evie says.

Gramps hands me a pebble from his pocket, to chuck in so we can hear how far down it goes before it hits water. We did it before, years ago, when Joe and I were little—made wishes of our own.

I lean over, let it drop. My head spins. I wait and wait.

'It's dried up,' I say.

'Or you just missed the splash,' Evie says. 'Come on, then.'

She and Gramps start walking. I fish in my pocket for something else to throw in: a tiny yellow cowrie shell, a safety pin, a five-pence coin. I slip them in, and with each I make a wish.

Let Mum and Dad be OK.
Let me be happy again.
Let me see Joe, one more time.
The darkness swallows them.

I run to catch up. Gramps is talking to Evie about setting the crab pots in the morning. 'You can come with me, Freya,' he says. 'Unless you are otherwise engaged, that is.'

'Of course she is,' Evie says. 'She won't be wanting to go out in that old rowing boat, just to get a few smelly crabs with you. Will you, Freya?'

I don't answer. I know the real reason why Evie doesn't want me going out in the boat. But I'm not going to argue now. And we're already back at the house, and there's a scrap of paper sticking out of the letterbox, with a message for me.

Eleven

It's scribbled in pink felt tip.

Hi Freya! We are all going down to the field later. Football then fire/barbecue on the beach. Please come. xx Izzy (+ Matt, Danny, Maddie, Lisa, Will, Ben, etc, etc)

Evie reads it over my shoulder. 'Sounds fun.'
'S'pose.'
'She's a lovely girl,' Evie says.
'Who is?' Gramps tips sand out of his shoes in a fine shower on to the garden path.
'Izzy. Isabelle. The girl helping Sally with the
53

campsite this year.'

'With hair like spun gold.' Gramps grins.

Evie sighs. 'You don't miss a trick when it comes to pretty girls, do you? See that, Freya? Not so muddled now, is he?'

Upstairs, I study myself in the mirror. Hardly spun gold, *my* hair. Nor ebony or anything else you'd find in one of those stories on Evie's shelves. I think of Mum, holding that mirror on the landing, the day before I left, how thin and faded she looked. It comes over me in a sudden rush, this overwhelming need to see her and talk to her, to *make* her see me. I almost pick up the phone, but I don't. I've tried it before. She'll be busy. She won't have anything to say. She'll start worrying. There's no point.

In the bath, I rinse off the sand and salt still stuck to my skin. My limbs look pale and thin in the dim light of the downstairs bathroom. Wearing my wetsuit on the beach today means I still haven't got that first flush of sunburn. I lie back in the water. Last summer, I could easily float in this bath but now I'm too long: my toes touch the end. I hold my breath and dip my head right under. Bubbles come out of my ears. My hair spreads out. I start counting the seconds. One, two, three . . .

What shall I wear for the beach party? We'll be playing football first, so jeans. Izzy will be wearing some crazy hippy thing as usual. And Matt will be there . . .

I imagine describing him to Miranda, even though I'm not intending to tell her anything right now because she'll just go on about it. Tall. Slim. Blonde hair that sticks up at the front, longer at the back. The bluest eyes. Wide smile . . .

54

I come up for air, spluttering. Someone's banging at the door.

'All right in there?' says Gramps. 'Not gone down the plughole or anything? Some of us lesser mortals need the lavatory once in a while, you know.'

'Sorry, Gramps,' I call back. When I stand up, water sloshes over the edge of the bath. I wipe it up with the mat. Start to towel myself dry.

How long was it that time? I lost count. I need a stopwatch.

I've got one, in actual fact. On the watch I use which was *his*, of course. The watch which has a compass and everything you need for navigation, and which he wasn't wearing either, along with the wetsuit that would have kept him warm.

*　　　*　　　*

Izzy waves as I come round the edge of the field. The game's already in full swing. I join her end of the pitch.

'Good you've come,' she says.

'Thanks for the note.'

'I looked for you earlier. Saw you'd all gone out. Nice time?'

'OK. Swimming and that.'

'Cool.'

'You?'

'Worked all day. Really busy. The campsite's packed.'

'Oi! Stop chatting!' Matt puffs past us after the ball. 'Come on! You're on our side, Freya.'

My cheeks go hot. Izzy doesn't notice. She chases after Matt and I'm left standing there like a loser, so I make myself run too. Danny waves to me from the other end of the field.

'Freya!' a voice calls.

The ball bounces past me and rolls into the gorse bushes at the edge of the field. I run after it. Matt gets there first and we almost collide.

'Whoa!' he says. He puts his hand on my arm, and all the rest of the game I can feel the place, like a burn. I know it's mad, but he's so totally gorgeous. Then Danny comes over and I forget about Matt for a while. He's caught a whole load of mackerel for the barbecue and he's dead proud of himself. He's OK, Danny. I like the way he gets enthusiastic about things. It's so *not* how most boys are, back home.

Danny's side win, but it doesn't matter. We play until the sun's gone down and it's too dark to see the pitch. Izzy and Matt have left already to start a fire on the beach at Periglis.

Some of the younger kids go back to the campsite. The rest of us join Izzy and Matt on the beach. We gather round the fire in a rough sort of circle. Danny comes over to sit next to me. We watch the sparks spiral-ling into the sky each time someone adds another log to the fire.

After a while, Izzy stops people piling more wood on. 'It needs to be white-hot for cooking, not flaming like this.'

Matt and Lisa lay sausages and burgers on a grill balanced between two rocks over the glowing logs. Danny adds the fish, tail to head alternately. He sprinkles herbs on them.

'Freshly picked?' I say.

He grins. ' 'Course.'

A dog comes nosing along the beach. It's Bonnie,

from the farm, snuffling out the crisps and bread people have dropped. She can smell the meat cooking. She comes when I call her, and sits right close to me, leaning into my legs. I smooth her head and she wags her tail in circles. Her ears are warm and silky under my hand.

Everyone watches Izzy. Her hair is frizzy from sea-spray, from the heavy dew that fell those last minutes on the field after the sun went down. It's spotlit by firelight, an orange glowing halo around her oval face. She's stripped down to a thin sleeveless T-shirt. Each time she leans forward, I glimpse the curve of her body. I can't help it. Matt sees too. Danny, Will, everyone. *Joe too, if he was here.* My skin prickles. I bend down and hug Bonnie.

Everyone helps themselves to food. Some of the older kids pass round cans. Some of them light up cigarettes. Danny and I go quiet, watching and listening. We're the youngest people left, now. The lighthouse beam goes round: two sweeping beams every twelve seconds, lighting up the rocks, guiding ships to safety. As the night gets darker, the beam seems stronger and brighter.

Matt and Will are talking about this theory that humans evolved from apes who lived in water, not land, and that's why we don't have fur and why we can control our breathing when we dive, and need to eat fish, and walk upright and stuff. I listen. It makes a lot of sense.

'It's late,' says Danny. 'I've got to get back.'

'Me too.'

Izzy gives us a little wave but no one else notices when we get up to leave. We walk single-file along the narrow footpath at the top of the beach, back to the campsite.

Danny peels off towards his tent. 'See ya!' he says. 'Sweet dreams.'

Electric light from the washrooms floods the top field. I make my way through the gate. After that, the lane seems extra dark. A dog barks as I go past the farm. My Tilly?

It's pitch-black, but not scary. The dark seems gentle and soft, folding round me. There's no wind, and no moon. The first part of the lane is overshadowed by the hawthorns either side, but as it goes up the hill the hedge falls away, and suddenly I see the sky above me like a huge canopy, studded by a million stars.

Nearly there. I can see the house.

Something light and feathery brushes my arm. For a second I hold my breath. *Joe?* But it's just a moth, flitting towards the light in the window. Evie never draws curtains. Who's to look in, after all?

She must have heard me come in. She calls from the top of the stairs. 'Everything OK? Did you have a good time, Freya?'

'Yes. Fine.'

'Night, night, then.'

*   *   *

I flick on the bedside lamp. Evie's turned down the sheet ready for me. There's a jug of flowers from the garden on the chest of drawers. Two pale rose petals have already dropped. A faint smell taints the room. Not the smell of stale water, something else. Different, but familiar, somehow.

A memory comes. Me and Joe, quite small, making rose petal perfume in the garden. We're

58

squashing the sweetly-scented petals into a jam jar, topping it up with water from the can in the greenhouse, stirring the pink mixture with a teaspoon. The next day the pink water has become sludge and is beginning to go brown, and each day it smells worse, stinky and foul and nothing like the scent of a rose.

Joe must be about eight. He's already too old for the game. He sneers at me. 'You didn't really think we'd be making real rose scent, did you?' *He'd* known all along it would go smelly and rotten. I'm furious. I cry.

I shut the memory out of my mind. I don't want to think about my brother like that.

You can't always do that so easily. Memories come back, pressing in on you, like ghost faces in the darkness pushing up against the glass, trying to get into the lit room. And sometimes the ghosts come in the night, in dreams, and there's nothing you can do to stop them.

Twelve

Last summer

The girl who arrived that day, August 14th, is sixteen. She comes from somewhere near Birmingham. Her mother (Lorna) is divorced. Her little sister's called Coral. Rosie makes friends with Coral.

Joe's like a lost person. He's fallen in love for the very first time.

'Hook, line and sinker,' Gramps says.

Gramps laughs when he hears what her name is. 'Samphire! It's a *plant*,' he says.

'Well, there's Ivy and Rose and Lily and all manner of flower names,' Evie says. 'The old names are coming back.'

'It's in Shakespeare, too,' Gramps says then. '*King Lear*.'

'No,' Evie says. 'You're getting muddled up now. That's Cordelia. The favourite daughter.'

'Samphire's in there too,' Gramps says. 'But as a plant, not a person. For picking and eating.'

They carry on like that for a bit, amusing themselves, but Joe doesn't think it's funny. He slams out of the back door, and goes to find Samphire (he starts calling her Sam, after that) for another *walk*, or whatever it is they do.

The first day after she turned up Joe showed her round the island, since she hasn't been here before. He wouldn't let me come, though. That's another thing that's new: before, all us kids just mucked in together.

I hear little bits and pieces about Sam. Scraps that start making a picture. Like the fact she doesn't like camping—never done it before. She's brought a different outfit for each day, but nothing warm enough, so Joe lends her his fleece. She starts using the bathroom at our place, because she doesn't like the showers at the campsite. She and Joe spend ages in his room.

That's where they are now. I'm lying on my bed in the room next door to them, writing in

60

my notebook. I wonder what Sam makes of the pictures on the wall next to Joe's bed: boats and lighthouses and fish and stuff. The map of shipwrecks, with the names and dates of the thousands of boats that have gone down around this archipelago (that's one of my favourite words at the moment). It's one of the most dangerous in the world, which is why Gramps has taught Joe about currents and navigation and sea-charts. He bought him a special watch with a compass and everything.

When I listen up against the wall, I can't hear a thing. No voices, or music, even.

*   *   *

Gramps clumps noisily up the stairs, whistling. He stops outside my door.

'Coming for an evening walk, Freya?' he calls. 'We'll stop at the pub.'

He knocks on Joe's door. 'Joe? Coming? Bring your friend, too.'

He's either forgotten her name, or he can't quite bring himself to say it. *Samphire.*

There's the sound of something scraping along the floor—furniture, or something heavy, before Joe opens his door a crack. 'Join you later,' he says, and he shuts the door again.

Through my open door I see Gramps just standing there, as if he's not sure what to do.

'I'll come,' I say. We go downstairs together.

In the kitchen, Evie purses her lips. She looks worried. 'What would Martin and Helen do?' she says. Helen is Mum, Martin is Dad, their son.

'About what?' I ask.

'Joe and that girl in his room all that time.'

I shrug. 'Nothing, I guess. She's just a friend.'

Evie and Gramps give each other funny looks.

'Sam is friends with everyone,' I say. 'It's fine.'

*　　　*　　　*

I think about this at the pub while Evie's ordering our drinks and Gramps is chatting to people outside. It's true that Samphire is friends with Joe and Huw, but not really with anyone else. She hardly speaks to me or the other girls, not even Lisa and Maddie. She doesn't join in the games on the field in the evenings with everyone else. She watches from the sidelines, looking bored. Sometimes I see her with Coral, washing up at the campsite sinks outside the stone barn, but mostly Coral plays with Rosie.

I know Evie and Gramps are worried, so for some reason that makes me want to reassure them. I take Joe's side every time, even though I am cross with him for spending so much time with his new *friend*. Now, sitting at the table outside the pub, I chat away so they don't keep wondering where Joe's got to.

He doesn't turn up, of course. At closing time we walk back in the soft dark, over the field and along the top of Periglis.

'Watch out for shooting stars,' I say. You always get them in August, when it's clear like this, if you look for long enough. Then you can make a wish.

I wish for the puppy. *Please let Mum and Dad say yes.*

*   *   *

Later, lying in the bath, I hear raised voices. My heart beats faster: it's so rare to hear Evie and Gramps arguing for real.

A door slams. I turn off the hot tap so I can hear better, but someone turns the radio on in the kitchen; classical music. I sink back into the water. I'm practising holding my breath. I want to be as good as Joe. Better. He can do nearly two minutes, he says.

When I come out of the bathroom the house is quiet. The bathroom is downstairs and you have to go through the kitchen to get to the stairs. The radio's off. Evie's reading in the front room.

'Nice bath?'

I nod. 'What happened?'

'Oh, nothing,' she says. 'Joe got a bit cross with us for interfering. We forget he's sixteen now. I suppose we're a bit fuddy-duddy. Old-fashioned.'

'No, you're not! You really aren't, Evie! Mum and Dad would've been much crosser, I expect, if he'd had a girl in his room all that time.'

Up in bed, I feel bad for saying that, as if I've betrayed Joe, somehow. I write about it in

63

my notebook before I go to sleep. *Sorry, Joe.* But he had it coming, really. He should think about the rest of us sometimes. Evie and Gramps and me.

Thirteen

It's mid-morning, the next day.

'Coming, then?' Gramps is pulling on his boots and waterproofs at the back door.

'You really don't have to go, Freya.' Evie says.. 'You know how cold you get on the boat.'

'I don't mind.'

'Mind you wear life jackets. Both of you.'

Gramps never used to bother. I wonder, briefly, as I go to fetch two life jackets from the hook in the shed, whether Evie blames him for Joe not bothering enough either. Except that when I think about it, Joe did. Bother, that is. He always wore a life jacket on the dinghy. Apart from that one time. It's just one of the things that doesn't add up. Doesn't make sense.

I follow Gramps out through the gate on to the lane. Two men are looking at the lighthouse buildings, holding clipboards. Gramps raises his hand in greeting as we go past.

'Estate agents,' he hisses, soon as we're out of earshot, as if they're a lower form of life.

At Periglis, we dump all the gear in the rowing boat and drag it down to the water together. Gramps lets me row. It takes a while for me to remember how to get the rhythm going, but I do. The tide's running out which makes it easier. To help with the rhythm, Gramps recites lines from Shakespeare:

' *"Full fathom five thy father lies;*
Of his bones are coral made . . ." '

As we get level with the end of the rocks the surface of the sea changes; out of the shelter of the bay the wind's whipping it up.

'Steady there. Here she comes.'

I brace myself as the wind slaps the side of my face. The boat rocks. A shiver goes down my spine. I think of Joe, out here in the dinghy by himself, in the dark.

'Left a bit,' Gramps says. Bit by bit he guides me out to the line of buoys and I hold on to the rope so he can start lowering the crab pots. I row from one marker buoy to the next, round in an arc. My arms begin to ache.

There are rocks all round here, which is why it's a good place to catch crabs. But you have to take care not to snag the boat: it's hard to see where the rocks are, at this point of the tide, when it's high enough to keep them covered. If you caught the boat on them, it would easily make a hole, and the boat would fill and sink in minutes.

'Could we swim from here?'

Gramps shakes his head. 'You're a strong swimmer. You might make it. But the tide would be pulling you out. It's further than it looks. It's always better to stay with the boat, if you capsize.'

We're both thinking about *Joe*, of course. The dinghy, upside down. The ache in the pit of my stomach shifts, moves under my ribs, to my lungs.

I lean over the edge, trail my hand in the green water. It's biting cold. Deep beneath, between the rocks, seaweedy forests sway, pulled by the invisible currents. It's so clear you can see tiny fish darting in shoals in and out of the forest, shadows moving in the darker patches beneath. When the surface smoothes I see my own reflection, a face peering back at me from under the water. I shudder.

'What happened to Huw?' I suddenly ask, just as Gramps is lowering the last pot. Evie was right about how cold it is out here on the water. My hands are like ice. 'Why isn't he working on the *Spirit* this summer?'

Gramps sits back in the boat and stares at me. The wind is making his eyes water. He doesn't answer. Maybe he didn't hear. Or perhaps he doesn't remember Huw. A seagull flies low over the boat. It sounds like it's calling the name: *Huw Huw*.

Gramps' breath sounds wheezy. He's sort of hunched over, a bit slumped.

'Gramps? Are you OK?'

He nods, straightens up a bit, tucks his raw red hands under his armpits to warm them up. 'Time to head back.' His voice is croaky.

I don't ask him about Huw again. His face is too red, and his eyes are watering; his breath labouring in his chest. He doesn't look right; perhaps he's got too cold. My own hands are freezing and my arms aching but I can't ask him to row, so I get back into position, pick up the oars again.

After a while, the splash of the oars dipping in and out, the trickle of drips from the tips of each paddle, begins to mesmerise me. My thoughts drift. I think about the world beneath us, down, down, down. Water washing stone, grinding it slowly into sand. There are stretches of sea-bed

66

between the islands which used to be valleys with village settlements, thousands of years ago. The sea level has slowly risen, covering it all up. Deep down, a whole flooded life is metamorphosing into something else. Fish swim through the places where houses would once have been; eels slither over ancient doorsteps. I imagine our boat gliding over empty rooms, sand drifting and burying the remnants of people's lives: old cooking pots, a small leather shoe, a string of beads. Sea levels are rising all the time. Faster now, with global warming and that. One day, this whole archipelago will be underwater. Nothing left.

A rubber dinghy with a noisy outboard engine swings into view. Their wash rocks our boat violently, so we have to stop rowing and cling on to the sides. Gramps yells at them and they swerve away. Someone waves.

'Some lads from the campsite,' he says. 'With diving gear.'

*   *   *

Izzy's on the beach at Periglis, watching us come in. She helps us bring the boat back up to the slipway and turn it over to let the water drain. She flirts with Gramps and he loves it.

'I'm just about to go over to Beady Pool,' Izzy says to me. 'Looking for stuff, if you want to come.'

I hesitate. I'm starving, for one thing, and then there's Gramps. But he seems fine now we're back on dry land. Only a bit wobbly. And there isn't much to carry back, just the oars and life jackets.

'It's all right. I'll be heading back home,' Gramps says. 'You two go and enjoy yourselves.'

We watch him walking slowly up to the path.

'He's cool, your grandpa,' Izzy says.

I nod. 'He goes a bit dreamy and odd sometimes.'

'I like *odd*,' Izzy says. 'More interesting. Come on, then.'

'I should stop off and get some food really. I'm starving.'

'We can go via the shop. I've got money.'

*   *   *

We spend all afternoon together at Beady Pool. The tide's ebbing, so there's the whole length of the sand and shingle for us to search along for bits and pieces for Izzy's jewellery. We spread our treasures on a flat stone to dry in the sun: pieces of turquoise glass smoothed by the sea; fragments of orange weed, like coral when they're dry; feathers; a skein of fine nylon rope, bright blue; shells with mother of pearl; tiny tortoiseshell cowries.

'I've looked a million times here for beads,' I tell Izzy. 'You know, like the beach is called after, from that shipwreck way back. How amazing that would be. You could charge the earth!'

'Our shells are just as pretty.' Izzy arranges them into patterns on the stone. She sits down on the sand, starts drawing with her bare foot. I watch her. I can't help it. I've been like this all afternoon. It's as if she trails magic after her. I want to know how she does it. It's something to do with the way she knows exactly what she wants to do, all the time. She's always in the present moment, not thinking about anything else. I wish I could be more like her.

68

She draws patterns and shapes in the sand, with the flat edge of a pebble. She draws a girl with hair like her own, but a fish's tail.

'So, Freya, why are you here by yourself? Where are your parents?' Izzy asks.

I explain about them working, and moving house, and how it's been the same most summers.

'They come over to join us at the end of the holidays, usually,' I start to say. 'Only this year . . . I'm not sure. Dad might come. Mum says she won't. They're not getting on very well. They hardly talk to each other. It's horrible. They don't tell me anything. I'm worried they're going to split up.' Just like that, I've blurted out all the stuff I've been bottling up for so long.

Izzy carries on doodling in the sand. She draws a house, gives it windows and a door, a chimney. She makes a pattern like roof tiles. 'It might not be as terrible as you think,' Izzy says. She adds a tree, and a garden fence with a gate, and a path up to the front door. 'My mum and dad split. I lived with my mum. The first two years she was sad all the time, but then we got used to it.' She smiles. 'You'll be OK, you'll see. And anyway, maybe you're wrong. Maybe it's just a difficult patch. All relationships have those, you know.'

It seems weird, thinking about Mum and Dad like that: in a *relationship*. As a couple, kind of separate from me and Joe.

'What about your dad, though? Do you still see him?' I ask her.

Izzy shakes her head. 'Hardly ever. His choice. His funeral.' She brushes sand off her hands.

Doesn't she mind? It fills me with misery, the thought of not seeing Dad. But he would want to see me, I know he would. He wouldn't let me go like that, so easily. Which means I'd have to live in two places, or choose between them . . . It's all too horrible to think about.

Izzy stops drawing. She sits back and looks at me. 'So. When's your birthday, Freya?'

'July.'

'What day?'

'10th. Why?'

'So you're Cancer.'

'What?'

'Your star sign is Cancer. Home-loving, sensitive, but with a hard shell, to protect yourself from getting hurt. Don't like change.'

'I'm not really into that stuff. Don't believe in horoscopes.'

'Don't you? What do you believe, then?'

I think for a bit. 'I'm not sure,' I say eventually.

Izzy's moved on to draw a merboy next to her mermaid, with hair a bit like Matt's. 'But you are sensitive, with a shell?'

'Suppose.'

She stops drawing a moment to look at me. 'I heard something about you. Least, I think it was you. Sally was saying something about last summer. An accident?'

'My brother died.' My voice cracks. I still haven't got used to saying those words. I'll *never* get used to saying them.

She leans forward, her voice sort of breathy. 'That's terrible. That's so sad. What happened?'

My heart's thumping. I have to keep swallowing. I can't speak.

Izzy puts her arms round me. She doesn't ask any more questions.

70

I cry softly, and Izzy just sits there, hugging me, for a long time.

*   *   *

It starts to get cold, sitting still. Izzy stands up, stretches. 'I think we should do something together,' she says, 'to free you from all this sadness.'

She starts smoothing a patch of sand next to the mermaid and the merboy. She draws the outline of another figure. It's like one of those chalk outlines in a detective film, to show where the body was, to begin with, but then she starts heaping up the sand, so that it looks like a body is actually there. After a while I can see it's meant to be me. She gives me seaweed hair and pebble eyes, and then she goes along the edge of the sea, looking for something. She comes back with a flat black pebble with a hole at the top, and she threads it on to a thin piece of nylon thread unravelled from a piece of old fishing net. She threads two small shells either side of the pebble, then ties a knot. She places the necklace on the sand version of me, then comes to stand next to me. She puts her arm round my shoulders.

'There you go,' she says, in her lilting voice. 'A talisman, to cure you of sadness. Now you will start to feel better.'

I almost believe her.

I *want* to believe her.

If only it could happen like that.

We stay there, not really talking or anything, but it feels nice, like something really special and important has happened between us. The sea

71

slowly ebbs. It leaves stretches of glistening silver sand.

*   *   *

We both look up when we hear voices. Two figures are making their way down the path to the beach. The spell Izzy has put over me is abruptly broken. I'm suddenly cold and hungry, and very, very tired.

'I'm going back now, ' I say.

'OK.'

I'm sort of expecting Izzy to come too, but she doesn't. That brief, intense conversation is already in the past. It's as if she's forgotten all about it now. She's moved on. She starts doing cartwheels along the beach, spinning further and further away.

I wave at her as I leave the beach.

'See you!' Her voice comes back faintly across the sand as she spirals away.

Almost as an afterthought, I snatch up the talisman necklace and kick the sand figure until it's just a pile of loose sand, then I start running back to Evie and Gramps' house.

It's late, much later than I'd meant to be. No one's in the kitchen, even though it must be supper time. I call up the stairs. 'Hello?'

Evie comes to the landing. Her face looks strained. 'Gramps isn't well,' she says. 'He's resting in bed now. Why didn't you come back with him? Where've you been all this time?'

'I'm sorry,' I say over and over. 'I didn't realise how late it was. Gramps said he didn't mind me going with Izzy . . .'

By the time she comes downstairs Evie's calmed

72

down. We make supper together and she takes a tray up to Gramps, and then we sit together in the front room.

'He'll be all right, won't he?'

'He's exhausted,' Evie says. 'He's all shaky. He's not talking sense, half the time. I'll phone the doctor in the morning.'

'Is it my fault?' I ask eventually.

'Of course not,' Evie says. 'You mustn't think that. I'm sorry I was cross before, when you came in. That was just worry, making me like that. Forgive me, Freya.'

I can't bear to see Evie like this. It makes me nervous. I can't settle. When Evie starts reading her book I go and stand at the window but we've already turned the lamps on, so all I can see is my own reflection in the glass and darkness behind.

'I'm going to bed.'

'OK, love. I'll be up shortly.'

I go along the landing to say goodnight to Gramps, but I can hear him, snuffling and snoring, already asleep, so instead I go further along, to Joe's door. I push it open and stand in the middle of the room, alone in the dark.

Someone's been in here: the window is open a little. I move forward, closer. The view through his window is the same as from mine, more or less. I can make out the dark shapes of trees and the black line of the sea, darker than the grey-black of the sky. The wind in the leaves makes a sound like water, and underneath, always there, is the rhythm of the sea itself, pounding the rocky shore.

Fourteen

Last summer

The summer wears on. It's unusually hot, day after day. Joe seems to be out all the time. Sam has stopped coming to the house for baths and stuff; she must've got used to the shower block or something. There haven't been any more arguments, but that's because Joe and Sam have stopped coming back to our place. I do the usual things—swimming, playing on the field, hanging out with the campsite kids and going on all the boat trips. A load of us buy snorkelling gear and we do that, down at Periglis. Me being so good at swimming means I'm as good at snorkelling as the older kids like Maddie and Will and Lisa. Sometimes Joe comes down and joins in, but mostly not. He goes running first thing most mornings, before I'm even up, comes back for breakfast and then disappears for the day. Occasionally I see him out on the fishing rock by himself, but usually Sam's there too, sunbathing with her eyes closed, leaning back against the warm rock face next to him.

Today I find him by himself. I go to the edge of Wind Down, clamber out to the rock you have to jump from. He makes room for me next to him on the fishing rock. He even lets me have a go, using the float I made with him at the beginning of the holiday. That seems

74

so long ago.

'Here,' he says. 'Like this.' He puts his hands over mine to show me how to cast the line and then wind it in, so the float darts through the water and the fish think it's something live, to eat. His hands are so warm and big, I want to cry, suddenly.

'I never see you,' I say.

'You're seeing me now, aren't you?'

He seems older, grown-up, even. His face is shadowed with fine dark stubble. His body is an amazing bronzed colour: he's hardly worn a top for weeks. He's not much like the brother I know, these days. It makes me feel younger than I actually am.

I try asking him about Sam. 'What do you two do all the time?'

He just looks at me with this funny lopsided grin. 'Nosy,' he says. 'None of your business.'

'Where is she now?' I ask.

'I don't know,' he says. A slight frown comes on his face, but he laughs it off. 'Fishing isn't exactly her thing.'

'How long is she staying?'

'Only a few more days,' Joe says. He wrinkles his nose.

Then he'll go back to normal. I can wait that long. She won't be here by the time Mum and Dad arrive, nor for the August bank holiday party, and I'm glad. Is that mean? Maybe it is. I should be pleased Joe's so happy. But Sam doesn't seem good enough for Joe. She's pretty and that; I mean, *really* pretty. She looks amazing. But she's not kind or

75

funny, as far as I can tell. Not interested in the things Joe likes. I can't think what they talk about.

When I text Miranda about it, she phones me straight back. She thinks she's such an expert when it comes to boys. She doesn't understand why I'm going on about it.

'He's in *love*, stupid! Talking doesn't come into it!'

Miranda says that, but I think it should. I think it *does* matter, that you're a nice person.

'Well, what do you know about it, Freya? Wait till *you* fall for someone, like *real love*,' Miranda says.

I can't imagine I ever will. I think about everything too much. I'm too picky.

*   *   *

That evening Joe has supper with us all. Evie's made shepherd's pie, and strawberry cheesecake for pudding. Afterwards, Joe comes with me to play football on the field. I'm allowed to be on his side. We play cricket next and I'm really happy because I bowl two people out (Lisa and Ben), and Joe and everyone on our team cheers. Lisa and Ben are fed up with me for ages. Sam isn't there. Neither is Huw.

We play out till long after dark. I love this night. I never want it to end. But it does, of course, eventually. Everyone walks back along the footpath to the campsite, and then just me and Joe go up the lane to our house.

'You go in,' Joe says. 'I won't be long.'

'Where are you going?'

'Not far. Go on, it's late. Evie and Gramps will be wondering where you are.'

'What about you?' I say. 'That's not fair!'

'I'm sixteen, for heaven's sake, Freya. I can do what I want.'

'No you can't!' I say, but I unlatch the garden gate.

I watch him carry on up the lane, until he's swallowed up in the darkness.

Lying in bed, I try to imagine where he might have gone. Up the lane, past the empty lighthouse buildings, and then where?

*   *   *

A few days later, and I'm retracing his steps. I don't know that for sure. I'm following my instinct, intuition, whatever. When you just know something without knowing you know it. I stop at the lighthouse buildings. The Keep Out notice pinned to the gate has faded in the sun and rain so you can barely read the words. Rust from the drawing pins has bled into the paper. I push open the gate into the overgrown garden. I haven't been here since that last time with Joe, weeks ago.

Someone else has, though. No one else would notice, but I see that the weeds growing over the path have been flattened by feet, and there's something different about the front door. That's it! You can actually see the door with its peeling blue paint. Before, there was this mass of prickly climbing rose and clematis growing right over it.

My heart's beating faster. I look over my shoulder. No one's there; just a bird calling from the hedge, and the sun still beating down, drawing out the smell of rank undergrowth. Butterflies flit from bush to bush. One shrub with blue flowers is covered in honeybees. Gramps' bees? For no good reason, that gives me courage. I step carefully over the squashed nettles growing beneath the front window and peer in.

Someone has definitely been inside. There's a small table where there wasn't one before, two rickety-looking chairs and a pile of rugs and cushions. If it was anywhere else, I'd have said a tramp or homeless person had moved in, but we'd have seen someone like that: on the island they'd stick out a mile off.

That's as far as I go, the first time.

I don't tell anyone. Not even Joe. I've got my secrets too.

*   *   *

The next time I visit, it's evening.

Joe hasn't been back to the house all day, but that's OK—we aren't having supper together because everyone's invited to the barbecue later in the evening, on Periglis beach. Evie and Gramps are busy in the garden. It's about seven in the evening. I find myself wandering up the lane, towards the old lighthouse. I'm not sure if I'm imagining it or whether there really is the smell of woodsmoke coming from the house. I can't see any smoke from the chimney. My heart's beating fast. I'm not afraid exactly, more like on edge, a bit excited, even. The gate's been left open. Someone's definitely been here before me. I creep in to the garden. All I'm going to do is look through the window. There's no harm in that, is there?

What did I expect? I'm not sure, thinking about it now. Is it spying, what I'm doing? Being nosy? I don't want anyone to see me, for sure. I sidle along the edge of the house to the window and peep in.

Samphire's sitting on one of the chairs at the table. The other is empty. She's looking down, smiling at someone out of my view. They must be sitting on the floor, on that rug. I realise how rare it is to see Sam smile like that. All her attention is on whoever it is in the room with her. She holds the long sweep of her hair back from her face with both hands and leans forward. She lets her hair fall softly back, and then she takes the hem of her skimpy T-shirt and slowly, ever so slowly, she starts to pull it up and over her head, still smiling, smiling. My first thought is: *She's undressing. What on earth for?*

Such a silly, childish thing to think! I know why really.

Heart hammering, I think: *Joe.*

It must be Joe, sitting on the cushions on the floor at her feet, watching every move she makes. She's taking her clothes off for him. This is what they do together.

I go dizzy. Quick. I've got to go, before they see me spying on them. Stupid, ignorant,

79

naive little sister.

An insect brushes my hand. It startles me. I shake it away, and as I turn I suddenly get a glimpse through the window of the person in there with Sam. It's not Joe. Relief floods through me. I duck down quick, and slink back along the wall underneath the window, round to the back of the house where there's no chance of them seeing me. I pick my way through huge rhubarb leaves and self-seeded cabbage plants and tall pink flowers with fluffy seeds in what must once have been the vegetable garden. I keep catching my clothes on things. Something stings my leg. At last I clamber over the stone wall and get back on to the lane. My heart's still thumping. No one saw me, though. No one knows.

As I get back to our house, it's beginning to dawn on me, what I've seen. What it means for Joe. Little by little, it becomes a weight, pressing down on my heart. I think about it as I pick the tiny, clinging burrs off my clothes. My leg is stinging and itchy with nettle rash.

Joe's beloved Sam was taking her clothes off for *Huw*.

What do I do now?

Tell Joe? Pretend I don't know? Say something to Sam? Or Huw?

It's none of my business.

I'm pretty sure that's what Miranda would say, or Maddie or Lisa or anyone else. Not that I'm going to tell any of them.

I hold the secret tight to me. All the rest of the evening and into the night, I can feel it there, a hand pushing down on my chest, stopping my breath.

Fifteen

I've been dreaming again. I wake with a start, all hot and muddled, because I can hear Evie talking on the phone, and I know from the tone in her voice that she's worried. *Gramps*, I think instantly. *Something's happened.* I lie in bed for a while longer, trying to work out from her voice just how bad it is. Then I hear Gramps calling out for her, and I can breathe again.

'The doctor's coming over,' Evie says when I go into the kitchen.

'Is he worse?'

'Same. Breathless. Muddled.'

'What can I do?'

'Nothing, love. You mustn't worry. I'm sure he'll be fine.'

I'm not convinced. I take a glass of juice out into the garden. The sun hasn't reached it yet; the shadows are long, and the grass is spangled with dew. It will be hot later. There's no wind. I prop open the greenhouse door like Gramps would normally do, and water the tomatoes and peppers in there. I love the smell of the leaves when you brush against them.

Gramps is propped up against the pillows when I go in to see him.

'Fern!' he smiles.

'Freya,' I say. 'I watered the tomatoes for you.'

'Good lass. You can get me the crab pots later.

81

They need checking today.'

Evie bustles in with a tray. 'No she can't,' she says. 'Whatever are you thinking of? We can't have Freya going out on her own in the boat like that!'

'I could ask someone else to help,' I say.

'Dave would do it, if he has a spare moment, when he's done the morning ferry. Would you go down and ask him later? And perhaps you could get some shopping, if I give you a list? I need to stay here with Gramps.'

'All this fuss,' Gramps says. He sinks back a bit, and his face looks too red against the white pillow. 'Tires me out.'

Evie shoos me back out of the bedroom. 'He needs to rest,' she whispers on the landing. Her hand is cold on my arm.

I'm thinking about yesterday, out on the boat. Why didn't I go back home with him? I could've carried all the stuff. It feels like it's my fault he's got this ill. What if something happens to him now? Joe first, then Gramps . . .

*   *   *

As I come over the ridge of the island I see the *Spirit* anchored out in the bay. The sea's still as a millpond, deep blue. I find Dave stacking boxes at the end of the jetty. A tractor-trailer is parked halfway down. The supplies boat must be due. I sort of hover, not wanting to interrupt, waiting for him to notice me. Which he eventually does.

'Freya,' he says, like a statement of fact. He keeps on stacking.

'Gramps sent me, he's not very well and he needs some help with the crab pots,' I say in a rush.

82

'What's up with him?'

'I don't know. The doctor's coming over.'

He stops, straightens up and frowns. 'Is this her?' We both hear the chug-chugging of a small boat engine coming round the headland, but it's not the doctor's boat. My face goes hot as I see who it is.

Matt steers his boat alongside the jetty and throws the rope for Dave to catch.

'Morning!' Matt says. 'Everything all right?'

'Freya here needs a hand to get some crab pots,' Dave says. 'Her grandfather's took ill. Can you do it, Matt? I've got the supplies boat arriving any minute.'

'Sure.'

Before I can say anything, Matt's got back in the boat and is making a space for me. There's nothing else I can do, is there? I haven't got a life jacket: Evie would go mental if she knew. But I get in anyway. Everything just falls into place and I go along with it.

No need to worry. There's not a breath of wind. The sea's like glass. But I guess everyone thinks like that, and that's when things go wrong. You never think it will happen to you.

'You'll have to show me where,' Matt says. He starts up the engine. It makes too much noise for us to be able to talk much, which is a relief. I just point which way to go. He knows about the rocks. I feel perfectly safe. I start to enjoy it: the blueness all around, the sun beginning to warm my back. Matt and me. Alone! I imagine telling Miranda.

As we come round the rocks towards the first buoy the light on the water is dazzling. I screw up my eyes. My face is wet with spray. Matt's boat is much faster than Gramps' old wooden thing.

'Here!' I say, and he cuts the engine. Silence folds back round us. The boat bobs on the waves. We work together, pulling up each pot to check for crabs. Most of them are too small, or the wrong kind and we throw them back. A crowd of squawking gulls starts following the boat as we move round the buoys. My hands begin to hurt from the cold.

'What shall we do with the empty ones? Leave them? Or bring them back?'

'I don't know. He didn't say.'

'We'll bring them all back,' Matt decides. 'Then he won't have to worry about them.'

In the end there's only a handful of edible crabs. It hardly seems worth the effort. But I'm not complaining really. I've spent all this time with Matt, just him and me, and it's easier talking when you're working together, somehow. He tells me about his dad's work on the Newlyn fishing trawlers. He talks about learning to scuba dive.

'I like snorkelling,' I say. 'That's all I've done, really. And a bit of free diving.'

'You should try it with oxygen,' Matt says. 'You'd love it.'

He pushes his fair hair back from his face. His eyes are shiny blue. I'm suddenly tongue-tied and embarrassed. Can't think of what else to say. If Izzy was here, she'd be chattering away, noticing things, making him laugh. I can't do that.

'OK, then, Freya? We'll head back, yes?'

He starts up the outboard. The gulls wheel off again.

I'm thinking of the way my name sounds when he says it. *Freya.* I look at his hand on the outboard, and the other on the edge of the boat. We don't speak. I want the journey to go on and on, not straight back to the jetty, but round the island, just me and Matt, and then we'll land somewhere, and swim, and maybe he'll teach me how to dive, and then we'll lie out in the sun . . . I hardly know what I want, and I know it's all wrong, me thinking like this, because he's Izzy's boyfriend. He's too old for me, and anyway it's all totally hopeless and silly. He probably thinks I'm just this little kid. He's only helping me because Dave asked him to, and because he's kind.

For the first time, I can just begin to imagine what it might have been like for Joe: how he might have been feeling about Sam, last summer . . .

We're back at the jetty. Matt's looking at me, waiting for an answer to a question I didn't hear.

'Sorry. What?'

'I'll bring the crab pots back to your place later, on the tractor, if you like? Save you carrying all this.'

'Yes. Thanks.'

He gives me a hand up from the boat. When he smiles down at me from the jetty, as I climb up the steps, my heart turns over.

'Thanks, Matt.'

'No problem.'

I force myself to keep walking without looking back.

Matt. I said his name, out loud.

He'll be coming round to the house later.

Stop it, I tell myself. *He belongs to Izzy. It isn't right.*

But I know Izzy can look after herself. She'd just laugh, if she knew. She wouldn't be worried. They're an item, a proper couple, Matt and her.

And anyway, how could I ever be in competition with Izzy? That's *really* stupid.

*   *   *

I almost forget to stop by at the shop, but just when I'm going past I hear voices from inside and it reminds me I promised Evie to get stuff for her.

It's Izzy's voice.

I go in; for a second it's too dark to see anything. My eyes adjust to the gloom: there's Izzy, leaning up at the counter, talking to the person at the till. Ben's dad runs the shop and post office. But it isn't him, or Ben, that Izzy's talking to.

'Freya!' Izzy beams at me. 'I guess you two know each other already? Huw?'

My heart stops.

Huw barely glances at me. He only has eyes for Izzy.

I hate the way he's looking at her. The way she's leaning towards him. I want to shout, or run away, or hit someone . . .

'I heard your grandpa's ill,' Izzy says to me. 'We saw the doctor's boat earlier this morning.'

'Should be getting back, to see how he is,' I mumble. I snatch up a wire basket and start putting in the things I remember from Evie's list. When I search for it in my jeans pocket my fingers close round the necklace Izzy made yesterday, on the beach. It didn't work, did it?

Except that I'm not sad. Right now, I'm furious.

Huw's still chatting to Izzy. Over the shelves of cereals and tins I watch his face. His fair hair flops over into his eyes and he smoothes it back. He's good-looking, but he knows it. Arrogant. It's all his

86

fault. If he hadn't been there, Sam and Joe might still have been together, and none of the rest would have happened . . .

And here he is all over again. Messing with Izzy now.

Does he sense me staring? He falters and is silent, mid-conversation. Is he remembering me, and last summer, and Joe? Feeling guilty?

Tea, filter coffee, orange juice, biscuits, eggs. I find the list, in the other pocket. Evie's written, *Treats?* What would Gramps like? Not beer or cake, if he's ill. I choose three ripe peaches and a bunch of red grapes.

I make myself go up to the counter. I put the basket on the side.

Huw starts taking the things out, weighs the fruit, prices it all up. 'Nine pounds and fifty-nine pence,' he says. He puts the shopping into a plastic carrier bag.

I keep my eyes down. I hand him a ten-pound note. He presses the change back in my hand.

'So, how are you, Freya?' he says.

His voice is different to what I expected: quite low and gentle.

He remembers everything. I know he does, in that instant.

'Got to get back,' I blurt out.

I know they'll both be watching me, will talk about me when I'm gone. I'm such a mess. It's all such a muddle. Suddenly it all seems like a terrible mistake, me coming back here for the summer. Raking up all the hurt.

I run in the back door, dump the bag of shopping on the kitchen table, run upstairs. I lie on my bed. Izzy's necklace in my pocket starts to hurt, pressed against my thigh. I take it out, dangle it in front of me. The shiny black stone has dried to a dull grey, but as it slowly revolves the light catches specks of crystal in it, like tiny stars. I hang the necklace in the window. Outside, the sky is a deep beautiful blue, but the day is spoiled now. I go back and lie on the bed for ages.

The house is deeply silent, as if it's empty. Gramps must be sleeping. Perhaps Evie is too. I don't go and check. I stay there on the bed, locked in my own misery. I don't even go down when I hear the tractor stop out in the lane, and the thud as the crab pots get dumped at the gate. The tractor starts up again: I let myself look from the bedroom window, but all I can see is the top of his head, his sun-bleached hair. It's all hopeless.

Why did Huw have to come back?

His part in things complicates everything, and now I have to think about that, too.

Eventually, I go downstairs. The shopping's all been put away in the cupboards. Evie's made food for us. She tells me about the doctor's visit.

'It's his heart playing up. The doctor's left some pills. He needs to take things very easy for a while, but he'll be fine.' Evie smiles, but her face is so tired and lined, big shadows under her eyes, she looks years older. 'I thought I'd invite your dad over, if he can take some time off work. That would cheer Gramps up, seeing Martin. What do you reckon?'

I'm not sure, suddenly.

'When?' I say.

'When he can get away.'

'Mum too?'

'If she'll come.'

88

'She said she wouldn't. Not ever again. Not here.'

Evie sighs. She flops down on a chair at the table, head in her hands. It scares me, seeing her look so. . . so *defeated*, somehow.

Evie looks up. 'Sorry, love. I'm just a bit tired. Look, why don't you go and have some fun, join the other kids this evening? I'm not very good company at the moment. I'm going to get an early night.'

I get it. She wants me out of the way. Fair enough. I can disappear, easy enough.

Sixteen

Last summer
August 25th

Joe came to the barbecue with everyone later last night, and at some point Sam turned up too, and I stopped worrying about them for a while, but this morning he didn't go running, and he didn't have breakfast, and I haven't seen him since.

I go with Maddie, Rosie and Coral to look for washed-up Venetian beads at Beady Pool, and then on to the sand bar. Maddie and I swim from the Gara end of the strand, and afterwards we sunbathe while Rosie and Coral play in the sand. It's just an ordinary day. We're getting used to it being sunny day after day.

Coral's nothing like her sister. I watch her.

She's fair, and shy and quiet. She smiles a lot at Rosie, sweetly. She doesn't seem to mind the way Rosie bosses her around.

'Here,' I say. 'Do you want these to go round the top?' I give her my handful of shells, to decorate her fairy castle.

She arranges them around the turrets. It's a good castle, for a little child. She's got loads of patience, unlike Rosie.

'What's your sister doing today?'

She doesn't answer.

Rosie pipes up instead. 'She's sleeping. In her tent. Then she's going to the pub like she always does.'

'She doesn't,' Coral says.

'Where, then?'

'I don't know,' Coral says. 'She doesn't tell me.'

'You should follow her,' Rosie says. 'That's what I'd do.'

Maddie laughs. She throws a pebble against Rosie's lumpy castle and it makes a big dent in one of the walls. 'You're such a nosy parker!'

'She's got a boyfriend,' Rosie says.

'We all know that,' Maddie says.

I lean over to help Rosie patch up the sand wall, so no one can see my blushing face.

*   *   *

I go back home the long way, via Periglis. The dinghy has been pulled up the beach, the sail rolled loosely round the mast, still dripping. That's where Joe must have been, then. It looks as if he was in a bit of a hurry. Gramps normally takes the sail right down, and brings the spare oars and all the gear back to the shed to dry off. I notice Joe's left the two bungs on the edge of the wall. He'll be mad if they got lost, or nicked, so I jump down on the shingle and go and pick them up, to take back with me. I find a washed-up sea-urchin too: pale purple and white stripes, almost perfectly round and whole. I start walking back along the path to the campsite.

Then I see them: two figures crossing the field. They go past the washrooms, through the gateway, up the lane past the farmhouse. I follow a safe distance behind. Sam has a bottle in one hand. Her feet are bare, she's carrying flip-flops in her other hand. She's wearing a short white skirt, and a black sleeveless T-shirt, and a black leather belt. Her hair hangs down her back like a glossy curtain; she could be a model, a girl in an advert. They stop outside the farm, and Huw goes into the house. Sam waits for him in the lane, so I have to go on, past her. She doesn't say anything and neither do I.

I push our gate open and stop, hidden in the garden behind the hedge. I hear Huw and Sam come past, on up the lane. I know where they're going now. I want to stop them right there, but I can't think how. All the time, I'm thinking about Joe. Imagining the hurt look on his face. The pain in his heart.

I go round the side of our house to the back garden. Voices drift from the downstairs bathroom: it's Evie and Gramps, now laughing softly together. I fetch the green rug from the sofa, take it back out to the grass under the apple tree and wait for Joe.

*   *   *

I look up when I hear his feet coming down the stairs: I know it's him, because of the way he always jumps the last three steps. He's been in his room.

'Are you going down the field?' I ask.

'No.'

'Why not?'

'I'm not going there,' he says.

'Where, then?'

'Out.'

So I follow him. Like Rosie said.

Up the lane.

My heart skips a beat.

Now all I can think of is that somehow I've got to stop him finding Huw and Sam. I can't bear the thought of him seeing what I saw.

He's almost there. He's lifting the stuck gate at the hinge end, to open it.

I sprint to catch him up.

He turns. 'What are you doing, following me?' He's angry. He grabs my arm and it hurts. I twist away.

'Go on. Scram.' He shoves me away.

I feel so stupid and helpless. There's nothing I can do. I watch him walk towards the peeling front door. For a second I'm paralysed: a rabbit caught in headlights, crouched behind the hedge. Blood thrums up the back of my legs.

More voices. Shouting. Joe comes skidding out of the gate and he bumps straight into me. He swears at me, shouts. He's nothing like my brother Joe. He hauls me up. His words spit into my face. 'You knew. You've known for ages, you deceitful little spy. Snooping on people.'

It's horrible. I start to cry. 'I only wanted to stop you, Joe!' I wail, but he pushes me aside and rushes off and in an instant it's all over.

I reason with myself as I wander back home. It's not so terrible. So, he found out about Sam and Huw. Well, better that he did, really. Otherwise he'd have gone on thinking how amazing and lovely she was for ever. Better to know the truth. Even if it hurts. The truth's always better.

I don't go straight home. I go across the island and past the church to the field, to see if Joe's gone there.

'Are you OK?' Maddie leaves the football game for a moment to talk to me. 'You're very pale,' she says. But my throat's sort of stuck: I can't answer, and I rush off again, her voice echoing after me. *Come and play, Freya! We need more people . . .*

I run along the shoreline path, jump down on to the disused lifeboat slipway. Once, each island had its own lifeboat and crew: nowadays, the lifeboat has to come from Main Island. Gramps' rowing boat is stacked upside down next to the slipway as usual, but the dinghy has gone.

I know instantly that Joe's taken it out. All the time I've taken wandering around looking

93

for him has been enough for him to get the boat down to the water, the sails up, and to make his way across the bay. I crane my neck, scanning the water. And yes, there it is: way beyond the rocky promontory, the white triangle of the sail. I can just about see it flapping as the boat catches a gust of wind.

I should call out, or wave, or something.

But he'll be all right. He knows what he's doing. It won't be dark for quite a while. Not really dark. Joe loves sailing: he'll come back feeling better. Everything will go back to normal. Only one more day and Sam will be gone, and we can forget all about her.

Seventeen

I try not to think about Huw. I reckon if I go and find Danny it'll take my mind off things. Usually, I like walking through the campsite in the evening. Everyone's cooking outside their tents, or sitting around chatting, and all the little kids race around playing games and it feels really relaxed. Once I've worked out Huw's not around, I begin to chill too.

I find Danny washing up at the outside sinks; I hang around with him while he finishes and help him carry bowls and stuff back to his tent, which means I get to meet his family. They are really friendly and easy and kind, so that makes a change from the rest of my day up till now. I end up staying ages. His dad makes me hot chocolate on their camping stove. Danny's little sister Hattie bullies me into reading a million stories. (Actually,

94

I like reading stories.) We read this big book of fairy stories, all in rhyme, and Hattie knows most of the words by heart. It's cosy sitting on a camping chair with Hattie leaning against me, all warm and ready for bed in her pink fleecy pyjamas, both of us sipping hot chocolate.

'Football now?' Danny asks. 'Coming?'

'One more story, Freya?' Hattie wheedles.

'Bedtime for you, Hattie,' her dad says, scooping her up and kissing her tummy till she squeals.

*   *   *

Danny and I walk together without saying much. I've cheered up a bit, though, and it's a relief to just lark about and run on the field. Neither Huw nor Matt are there. Izzy says they're helping Dave with some boat trip, at Bryluen. She's on the other team so we don't get to talk much. She asks me how Gramps is, but that's all.

We play out till it's too dark to see the ball. The younger kids drift back to the campsite. I sit in a circle with Danny, Izzy and the others, chatting about not very much. Maddie and Lisa decide to go to the pub. Izzy doesn't want to go. In the end it's just Danny, Izzy and me left.

'Let's lie down and look at the stars,' Izzy says.

'Why?' Danny says.

'Just do it and see.'

So we lie down. The grass is slightly damp. Above us, the sky is clear and studded with stars. The more you look the more you see. After a while it seems as if the sky is pressing down, heavy with a million trillion stars each of which is a tiny pinprick but together making a whitewash of light. The sky

95

seems to curve, pulled down to earth at its edges. You can see how the earth is actually round. I've never noticed that before.

We point out the constellations we know: the Great Bear and the Plough, Orion the Hunter and Sirius, the Dog Star.

'Wish we had a telescope,' Danny says.

'Why? You can see everything like this. You're more part of it. Isn't it amazing?'

'Yes,' I whisper. It's mind-blowing. Extraordinary.

Danny keeps fidgeting.

'Sshh! Listen,' Izzy says. 'They make a sound.'

'What do?'

'The stars.'

'How come? That's impossible,' Danny says.

'Just listen.'

There *is* a sound. A very faint, high-pitched fizzing, like static. My head starts to spin.

'The music of the spheres. Zinging down to earth, to us.' Izzy's voice comes out all breathy and awesome.

Danny sits up. 'Ugh! This grass is sopping wet!' He stands up and stares back down at me and Izzy. 'You are almost the same colour as the field.' He walks a few paces away. 'From here you are invisible. Someone could walk right over you.'

Izzy laughs.

My head swims. I'm drunk with starlight. I feel tiny, under this vast sky. So many stars, and some of them aren't even there any more, already burned up, even though their light is still travelling towards us, to this moment. It's taken that long: light years. Out loud I say the word *firmament,* not because I'm religious or anything, but because it's

96

such a lovely word, and it feels like this sky needs an amazing word.

'What?' Izzy says.

'Firmament. The sky.'

Izzy says it too.

'Hey, Matt's coming this way,' Danny says. 'Stay quiet and see if he notices you.'

But Izzy giggles. 'Hi, Matt. All finished, then? Boat sorted?'

Matt looks slightly bemused, staring down at Izzy. 'Coming for a drink? Huw and Luke are there already.'

'Not tonight. You can.'

'Not bothered. I'll go back with you.'

'We're not going back. Not yet. Lie down and watch stars with us.'

'I'm off,' Danny says. 'Coming, Freya?'

'Don't go yet!' Izzy holds on to my sleeve.

So I don't. I do what she wants, because I want it too. That's the effect Izzy has.

Danny looks a bit fed up. He doesn't say bye or anything. We watch him disappear into the dark.

'Ahh!' Izzy says. 'He really likes you, you know?'

'Shut up!' I push Izzy away lightly and she laughs.

Matt comes and joins us. He lies down in the space between Izzy and me. I feel tingly and weird being so close. I can sense his body like heat, even though he's not actually touching me. Above my face the air feels cold now.

His clothes rustle as he turns towards Izzy to kiss her. I know that's what's happening without seeing any of it. I seem to feel it, almost. The brushing of fingertips. Lips.

I'm totally still, silent, bathed in starlight.

'Shooting star!' Izzy says. 'There!'

97

'A comet, more like,' Matt says.

'No, shooting star: rock, hurtling through space towards earth. One day there will be a huge one, big enough to obliterate Earth completely.'

'Cheerful, aren't you, Izz?' Matt says.

'It's the truth. Everybody knows it.'

'But right now, scientists round the world are busy working out ways to deflect it, change its course or blow it up before it gets here.'

'That's what they like to think,' Izzy says. 'Some people like to think they can control everything. It terrifies them if they're not in control. What do you think, Freya?'

'I don't know. It's complicated. I guess no one likes to think about all this ending—this planet, I mean. But we all do have to end, sometime. Like, individually. We're all going to die one day, whether we like it or not.'

'Not,' Matt says. 'Not yet, not for a long, long time.'

'You don't know,' I say. 'No one does.'

We're all quiet for a bit. I imagine Izzy nudging Matt in the ribs, to shut him up.

'What if we die, but it's not the end? What if we just change?'

'Into what?'

'I'm not sure. Not ghosts, exactly. More, like, a spirit you, which doesn't need a body.'

'Your soul?'

'Yes. Something like that.'

'Dust to dust, ashes to ashes. Everyone's made of stardust, did you know that?' Matt says. 'All matter originally comes from the stars. So you, and me, and Freya, we're all made of stars really.'

Stardust. I like that.

98

That dust to dust stuff comes from the funeral service. They make you think about it, in the church, and afterwards too, for the burial. I swallow hard, blink back the tears that come like an automatic reaction when I remember back to that horrible day. Sometimes I wish it had been at the little island churchyard rather than the bleak town cemetery back home. Joe's friends, sixteen-year-old kids from school, in tears, standing around awkwardly.

Izzy stands up, starts walking away across to the edge of the field. For a few precious minutes it's just Matt and me lying on the wet grass, side by side. I hardly dare breathe. I keep totally still and stare at the stars. Matt moves his hand, ever so slightly, towards mine. Touching mine, even. Although afterwards I can't really be sure. In any case, it was just by accident. It didn't mean anything.

So why do I keep thinking about it, as the three of us walk slowly back to the campsite? And when I get home, and climb into bed, why do I put my other hand on the place he touched, as if he's left a mark there? Why do I hold it all night?

I lie under the faded quilt, my body burning with new feelings, aching with longing for something I can't have . . .

Was it like that for you, Joe? With Samphire?

Eighteen

Sand trickles on to the floor when I pull on my jeans the next morning. I peer at my face in the mirror: freckles all over my nose, hair sticky with salt, frizzy from last night's damp air. I stick out my tongue at my reflection. No one is ever going to look at me the way Matt looks at Izzy. Why would they? Stupid me, getting all worked up like that. Matt belongs to Izzy. Izzy is my friend. End of story.

I wonder what Mum and Dad are doing right now. It's about nine; they could be waking up together in their big bed, drinking tea, planning a day out, just the two of them . . .

More likely Dad left early for work, and Mum's listening to Radio 4 in the kitchen, staring at the walls and trying to summon up some energy to unpack the boxes still untouched in the empty rooms in the rented house. Perhaps they've already decided to part: that's why she let me come here for the summer, so she and Dad can sort it all out, and when they see me at the end of the summer they'll tell me it's all decided and there'll be nothing I can do about it. Perhaps she's leafing through house details, small poky houses in the cheap end of town near the station, which is all she'll be able to afford with her share of the money from the house sale. And Dad . . .

Just a difficult patch, Izzy said. *Everyone has those. It might not be as bad as you think . . .*

Miranda says I have this habit of exaggerating things. It is true that sometimes I do imagine things

100

so vividly I start to believe they must be true. And I have been spectacularly wrong in the past. But the opposite is also true: that I see what I hope to see, sometimes, and convince myself that things are better than they actually are. Which leaves me precisely where?

Nowhere, of course. *Stop thinking, Freya.*

I fish out the stash of postcards I keep tucked in my notebook. I choose one with a picture of the standing stone on Gara: it's important there's no sea in the picture, no boats or anything to set Mum off, and I start to write.

Hi Mum and Dad
Thinking about you. Hope the move went OK and you like the new house and everything. Miss you.

I cross out *and everything.* I re-read the rest. My words sound distant and empty. I can't begin to tell them what it's like here this summer. I wish I could tell Mum about the dreams, and the remembering, and what it's really like being here without Joe. I realise it's days since I spoke to either of them.

*   *   *

Soon as I've posted the card I start walking towards the maze on Wind Down. It's not beach weather, though it might be later, if the sun manages to burn through the sea mist. It suits my mood: soft grey light, muffled sounds. Every so often the fog horn booms out over the island. You wouldn't want to be out in a boat in this. My feet take me round, back, round, in towards the centre of the labyrinth. I close my eyes and sway, slightly.

My questions about Joe's accident have been in my head for so long it's wearing me out. It's building in my skull like a pressure, like a physical weight pushing down. I don't know how to stop it or let it out. I wonder if it feels like this when you're going crazy. Am I? *Crazed by grief*: I read it, somewhere. It really happens. I'm still no closer to an answer.

I carry on walking across the downs, along the cliff edge, seeing how close I can get, checking how easy it'd be to step over in a mist like this. But it's not hard to tell when you get close: the air quality changes, and there are gaps in the mist, and it's not so dense now anyway.

It's quite strange, walking into the white-grey dampness. It closes in around me. I've no sense of being on an island now: I can't hear the sea even though I'm so close. Droplets of moisture cling to my hair and my clothes. I feel separate, totally alone.

It's not exactly spooky but my senses are all on edge, maybe because the usual clues aren't there. And perhaps that leaves me wide open to what happens next. Perhaps it explains why I don't freak out or anything, when I see a figure, down on the rocks.

This time I know it isn't Danny, even though he's about the same size. This time it's a completely different feeling from before, when I thought I saw him fishing from the rocks at Periglis. It's what I've been waiting for, longing for, ever since I arrived on the island. I know, clearly and absolutely, that it's Joe. But it's not like I expected.

He's wearing his old blue jacket, the collar

turned up. He's got his hands in his pockets, and he's jumping from rock to rock, going along in the same direction as me. Because of the mist, I see him in snatched glimpses. We're walking in parallel, me up here on the cliff, and him below at sea level. It's my brother Joe exactly like he was last summer before anything happened. There's nothing *hurt* or *damaged* about him.

I'm not going to ask how this can happen. I'm not going to call out, or run up and touch him, or anything like that. I just keep walking steadily on, and looking, each time the mist swirls and clears a gap, and gradually this extraordinary feeling of calm comes over me.

He is all right.
I haven't lost him for ever.
He's here, with me.

He doesn't look up. There's nothing to show he's noticed me, even, although I'm totally sure he knows I'm here. It's *why* he's there, of course. And then, the next time the mist clears enough for me to see, I realise he's disappeared again. He's not there any more.

I won't ever tell anyone else about this. I'm not going to let them say *you imagined it, Freya: of course there was nothing there. How could there be?* People too easily take things away from you that *they* don't understand and can't explain.

By the time I've gone past the fishing rock, the mist has begun to lift. The sounds come back too: gulls, the murmuring of water on stone, the *chit chit* sound of a bird tapping a shell against a rock. I find a sheltered place to sit, and lean back against the wind-smoothed side of a granite boulder. I close my eyes and breathe in the sweet smell of damp grass and crushed wild thyme.

Thank you, Joe.

I sit there thinking about him for a long time. I stop feeling the cold air and the damp, even. It was him. He came. He was fine. Is that what it means? He was showing me he's all right? That I can stop worrying about him?

*   *   *

'Hey! Freya!'

Danny's mooching along the path, fishing rod and bucket in hand. His voice breaks the spell. I've been sitting there by myself for so long I'm pleased to see him, though I don't let on. The mist has almost completely cleared.

'You're all wet!' he says. 'What are you doing?'

'Just sitting.'

'Did you hear the fog horn, earlier? Warning ships?'

'I did.'

Danny sort of hops one foot to the other, a bit nervous. 'Want to do something?' he says.

'Like what?'

'I don't know. Just hang out together, I guess.'

I shrug. 'If you like.'

'Where shall we go?'

I stand up. I've been hunched there for ages and my legs feel all tingly and weird. It makes me laugh.

'What?'

'Pins and needles.' I explain. 'From sitting still too long.'

I get an idea, suddenly. 'If you want,' I say, 'I'll take you somewhere special. As long as you

104

promise to keep it a secret. *If* I can find it.'

'OK.' He sounds a bit wary, doubtful.

'You'll have to follow behind me, once we find the path. It's very narrow.'

Path is a bit of an exaggeration. You'd never find it in a million years without someone showing you. I first came here about three years ago with Joe. I find it eventually, by a sort of instinct, clambering along the big rocks, ducking under a stone arch and squeezing through the narrow gap between two huge boulders. It's a bit like caving except not underground: there are places which are so narrow you have to suck your breath in and half crawl. I was smaller—shorter—last time I came. It's more difficult than I remember.

Danny's huffing and puffing behind me, protesting.

'Trust me,' I say, turning back to grin at him.

We come out on a ledge about halfway down the cliff, and edge along that, round the next curve, and then at last we can drop down another level on to granite rocks, just above a narrow inlet which at low tide makes a small triangular beach of silver sand, totally hidden except from the sea. And on this side of the island you hardly ever see boats close in. It's much too dangerous.

I jump the last metre or so and Danny follows. Our feet leave deep prints in the wet sand.

'Wow!' Danny says. 'Amazing!'

'Worth the effort?'

'Definitely.'

We take off our shoes. You can't possibly stay wearing shoes on a pristine, perfect beach like this, where you're the first people to leave footprints. We run around a bit crazily and then flop down in a heap, breathless.

'How did you find *this* beach?'

'My brother found it. We never saw anyone else here, ever. We've never told anyone about it. So you must keep it a secret.'

'Of course!' Danny's face glows. He looks at me and smiles, properly. 'Thanks, Freya!'

The sun's beginning to burn through the low cloud.

'Should've brought swimming things,' Danny says.

I pick up a pebble and start drawing patterns in the damp sand. Danny finds a funny bit of seaweed like a donkey's tail and tries to stick it on me, and we end up having a seaweed fight, and get covered in sand. I laugh and laugh and it feels brilliant. We roll our jeans up and paddle in the shallows. I love the feeling of the water running back out under my toes. Danny finds a crab and then I do too and we try and make them have races, only they just make for the nearest rock and hide.

We poke around in the rock pools. We sit next to the biggest one, side by side, staring in.

'I heard about your brother,' Danny blurts out.

I poke at a sea-anemone, feel its tentacles pulling at my finger, trying out if I'm edible. I bite down on my lip, hard.

Danny's shadow falls over the pool and a tiny sand goby flashes back under the weed. 'Izzy told me. I wanted you to know that I knew, if you see what I mean. Like, I didn't want it to be secret.'

'What did she say?'

'Not much. That your brother was in some sort of accident, and he died, and it was only last year.' Danny looks at me, waiting.

Normally I'd clamp up right there and then. Run off. Something. But I don't. Maybe it's because of what happened earlier, in the mist. Or maybe it's because we're sitting together on this secret beach which is mine and Joe's special place, and I feel safe. Or maybe I'm just ready, at last, to speak about it instead of keeping it all locked in my own head, going round and round and round.

I start to tell Danny the story. Just the bare bones, what happened on the last evening. And it isn't hard, not once I start.

Nineteen

Last summer
August 25th still

I go back to the house, since there's nothing else to do.

Evie calls down the stairs. 'Freya? Joe?'

'It's me,' I call back.

Why don't I tell her what Joe's doing? Later, I ask myself this over and over. I still don't know the answer.

'Gramps and I are having an early night,' Evie says. 'Help yourself to food or whatever. And can you bring the chairs in from the garden? I forgot. Thanks, love.' She closes their bedroom door. It's only about nine o'clock!

I can't seem to stay still. After I've put the chairs in the shed and brought in the rug I wonder about going back to the field to play. I can't stop thinking about Joe. Upset, because of Huw and Sam but also because of me. Out there on the boat. It doesn't feel right. Then I think of something and my heart lurches. I go back out to the shed to check: Joe's wetsuit and all four life jackets are still hanging there.

Still I don't wake up Evie and Gramps. Maybe because of that note in her voice earlier: *don't disturb us*. I'm halfway along the path to the field when my hand feels something in my pocket and I realise with the most awful gut-wrenching, stabbing pain that I've still got the boat bungs, which means that not only has Joe taken the boat out without wearing any safety equipment for himself, he hasn't even checked the boat. As he goes out into the bay, sea will gradually seep into the hold and weigh down the boat, making it lower and lower in the water, and more and more difficult to control. Panicking now, I start running.

Luke, Ben and Maddie are the first people I reach at the edge of the field. I start gabbling about Joe.

'Hey, chill,' Luke says. 'Slow down a bit.'

But Ben understands. Alarm registers on his face too and he's running to tell Huw . . . *Huw* of all people!

'He isn't wearing a life jacket,' I say between gulping sobs. 'Not a wetsuit even, and it's getting dark and he hasn't got lights or anything.'

'He'll be all right,' Luke says. 'He's been out in that boat a hundred times before. He knows what he's doing.'

'But this is different. He was really upset,' I start to say. But by now Huw's come over so I don't explain properly about that either.

Huw goes into action mode immediately. I hate him and I am enormously relieved all at the same time.

'Run and get your grandparents. Quick! Now!' he instructs me. He's got his mobile out and already he's pressing the numbers for the coastguard.

That's how the nightmare begins.

*   *   *

It isn't long before we hear the engine of the lifeboat coming from Main Island. I'm freezing cold, shaking all over.

It'll be all right now. It will find him easily. He can't have got that far. Even if the tide was pulling him out, he knows the waters well enough, where the rocks are and everything. Any minute now and we'll see them towing the dinghy back in . . .

Gramps and Evie are already up and dressed and running along the path towards Periglis by the time I get down there. Huw must have phoned them already. I have to go over my story again and again, like I do later to the coastguard, until I'm so weary and muddled it hardly makes sense. I tell them about the bungs.

'It isn't your fault, Freya,' Evie tells me over and over. 'That stupid, stupid boy. Just wait till I get my hands on him. I'll kill him, I swear I will. Without a life jacket! What was he thinking of? And in the dark, for heaven's sake!' She's crying too. I know she's being cross because she's so scared and it frightens me even more.

Gramps goes white and quiet. He's all for taking the rowing boat out, and Huw and Dave offer to go out in the *Spirit*, but the lifeboat men won't let them. The wind's got much stronger. The tide's running fast. They don't want to be doing two rescues, or more.

After a while Evie makes me go back to the house with her. That's when we first hear the helicopter, circling over the island and back and forth across the Sound. Its searchlight beams out over the black water.

I know it's very bad news. The coastguard's called the Air Sea Rescue because the inshore lifeboat hasn't found Joe. It's pitch-dark now. How can they not have found him? It doesn't make any sense. Surely a searchlight would pick up the white sail easily enough?

*   *   *

We're all huddled in the sitting room when the phone rings. Evie jumps up. Her eyes are circled with purple shadows. I feel sick and faint. Gramps just stands at the window, like he's been doing for nearly three hours now, hands in his pockets and jingling the coins in there. The sound's making everyone even more on edge.

Evie repeats the coastguard's words.

'They've found the dinghy.'
Gramps turns, relief flooding his face.
Why isn't Evie smiling?
'But not Joe.'
All the colour drains from Gramps' face.
My palms are sticky with sweat. Blood thumps in my skull.
'The boat had capsized.'
Evie collapses on to the sofa next to me. Gramps takes the phone from her hand. His knuckles are white against the grey plastic.
Evie starts to rock, head in her hands, making a strange sound.
She gathers me into her arms and tries to rock me with her.
Still I don't cry. I'm stiff, sort of frozen.
It's my fault. All of it.

*   *   *

The helicopter and the lifeboat get called off at about one, because it's too dark and the wind's gusting to storm force. They'll resume the search at dawn. Gramps goes out: Evie doesn't even try to stop him. He goes down to the bay, I find out later, and waits there all night. Sally from the farm comes to sit with Evie and me. No one says much. Sally makes tea which no one drinks. At some point, Evie must have phoned Mum and Dad, but I've blotted that out of my memory.
At about five, we walk down to Periglis. The wind has blown itself out and it's a beautiful cool summer morning, the sky all peach and pearly. Gramps isn't there. Eventually, we find

111

him at the end of the jetty: he's walked out to meet the police boat which is just making its way across from Main Island.

Twenty

Danny listens while I talk without interrupting once or jumping in with his own stories about accidents, like people sometimes do. But perhaps this time I've talked too much, because he doesn't say anything at all, for ages.

The sun shifts round the little beach so we're in shadow again and it's chilly. When I finally stand up, my legs hurt from being crouched down so long.

Danny throws a limpet shell into one of the rock pools. The rings spread out across the surface. 'Can I ask you something?' he finally says.

'Of course. What?'

'Why did you think it was your fault?'

'Because if I hadn't picked up the boat bungs he'd have seen them on the wall and realised he needed to put them in. Because me following him to the house and then hiding in the lane made him even more angry and upset. Because I should have stopped him going out on the boat, and told someone straight away. Isn't it obvious?'

'No.' Danny frowns. 'Still doesn't make it your fault. I don't see that. He was responsible for what he did. Not you.'

It sounds as if he's blaming Joe, but I know he doesn't mean it like that, and he's trying to be kind to me.

112

'We all felt like it was our fault. Gramps did, Evie, too. They were supposed to be looking after him. But I was the one who knew what was going on. So it was more my fault than anyone else's.'

I hesitate. Shall I tell Danny the rest? I've come this far, I might as well tell him everything.

'To begin with I felt sure it was my fault. Lately, I've started wondering something else. Something worse.'

'What?'

'Whether Joe did it on purpose. *Meant* to do it.'

'Like . . .'

'Deliberately. It wasn't an accident. He made it happen. Didn't do the safety checks. All that.'

'But why? Why would he do that? That's just crazy, Freya.'

'Is it? *Really*? Because otherwise it just makes him stupid. And Joe definitely wasn't stupid. He knew about boats, and safety drills, and weather conditions. About tides and winds and currents and the rocks in the bay.'

'But what would make him do such a thing? I mean, you'd have to be really, totally desperate, to want to drown. To take your own life. That's pretty extreme. If that's what you're saying.'

Danny's words sound so blunt and horrible. But that is the heart of it. What might have happened, to push Joe that far? Is finding Sam and Huw naked together enough? Even if she was the first girl he'd fallen in love with, even if he was totally head over heels besotted with her? He'd only known her a couple of weeks. I rake through everything I can remember. Did he seem, like, fed up? But I hardly saw him, those last weeks. And before, he was talking about his plans: leaving home, that course, adventures. It's not like someone who's going to take his own life, is it?

'I'm trying to work it out,' I tell Danny. 'That's why I keep going over and over it in my head, what exactly happened, remembering everything bit by bit, trying to make sense of it all. Kind of looking for clues. It's like there's a piece missing.'

Danny fiddles around with a piece of seaweed. He chucks pebbles at a rock. He gets up and wanders down to the sea and stands staring at it for the longest time.

I shiver. 'Shall we go back?'

He nods. When he turns round his face is in the shadow. I can't see his expression.

'I'm sorry I landed all that on you,' I say. 'I know it's pretty heavy stuff.'

'Don't apologise,' Danny says. He sounds almost fierce. 'I'm glad you told me.'

'Thanks.'

'What on earth for?'

'Listening.' I shrug. Now it's me who's embarrassed.

'Sorry if I didn't say the right things.'

'You did fine. There aren't any *right things*, in any case.'

We start the climb back up the rocks. 'You won't tell anyone about any of this, will you?' I say. 'Not about the secret beach, and not about Joe, either.'

'OK.'

'Promise?'

'Promise.'

*   *   *

As we clamber over the rocks and along the ledge,

through the passage between the wind-carved boulders, it seems as if each twist and turn takes us back into something more ordinary and everyday. It's a relief. The heavy feeling in my heart begins to shift. By the time we get back to Wind Down we are talking about the usual things: having another barbecue, and whether or not to go snorkelling on Bryluen. We go through the wicket gate into the top field. His sister Hattie waves from their tent.

'Want to come back to ours for tea?'

I nod.

*   *   *

The kitchen stinks of fish.

'There you are!' Evie says. 'I was beginning to wonder.'

'I had tea with Danny's family,' I say.

'That's nice.'

'Yes. What are you cooking?'

'Crabmeat. Sorry about the smell.' Evie lifts a pan from the stove and puts it on to the table. 'Gramps has been asking for you.'

'How is he?' I feel bad that I've hardly thought about him all day.

'Much better. Still needs to rest, but he looks brighter. Go up and see him.'

He smiles when I put my head round the door. 'Hello, stranger!'

His face still looks grey against the white pillow. I go right in and take his hand.

'You're all wind-blown,' he says. 'You smell of the sea.'

'That's the smell from the kitchen!' I say, wrinkling up my nose. 'So, are you better?'

'Getting there.'

'Do you want anything?'

'You could bring me up some honey,' Gramps says.

'What, on toast or something?'

'By itself, with a spoon.'

'Hang on, then.'

Jars of honey from Gramps' bees are lined up along the shelf in the kitchen cupboard. They glow in the evening light, as if each pot is full of sunshine. I take out one that's already been opened and carry it up to Gramps.

He takes sips of it from a spoon. 'Like medicine,' Gramps says, smacking his lips. 'It's healing, that honey. Those bees know a thing or two.'

I stay there a bit longer, to keep him company. He closes his eyes after a while and I'm about to tiptoe out when he says, 'This fine weather won't last.'

'No?'

'Make the most of it, while you can.'

'I am. I might go snorkelling with Danny.'

'Danny?'

'One of the boys camping this year. The one who looks a bit like Joe.'

Gramps opens his eyes. They're all pale and rheumy. 'You be careful.'

Perhaps I shouldn't have mentioned Joe. Gramps' voice sounds shaky and old, suddenly.

'It's not natural, breathing underwater,' he says.

'It's perfectly safe,' I say. 'You don't go deep, like diving. You have the mask and tube. You know that, Gramps.'

He tuts.

'But I won't do it if you don't want me to.'

Gramps dabs his hand in the air, trying to catch at a fly that's buzzed in through the open window. He sighs. 'Don't take any notice of me,' he says. 'I can't keep you wrapped in cotton-wool for ever.' He sits up a bit more against the pillow. 'I think about him every day, you know,' he says. 'I go over everything I said to him, those afternoons I was teaching him to sail.'

'Oh, Gramps!' I've a lump in my throat.

'I've gone over and over it in my mind that many times. It doesn't make any sense. I can't work out why it went so badly wrong. How he could have forgotten everything, like that. What made him so . . . so careless.'

Evie comes in with a tray. She takes one look at Gramps. 'You've worn yourself out, Bill! Better let him get some rest, now,' she says to me.

I lean over to kiss his papery cheek.

Gramps smoothes my hair. 'Life's precious, remember,' he says. 'Make the most of it. Don't take any notice of me.'

*   *   *

Instead of going to my room, I sit in Joe's, writing in my notebook. It sort of brings him closer, sitting with his things round me. My pen scratches a tiny figure in mid-jump from one rock to another. *Did* I see him, this morning? And if I did, what does it mean? Is he really here, on the island? Not a ghost exactly. Not just a memory . . .

I was so sure at the time, but already it's beginning to seem like something else I might have imagined. I'm glad I didn't tell Danny about it.

I think about all the things I *did* tell him. I don't

know what came over me. But it was OK, really, how he reacted and everything. It's weird to think how just one summer later there's a whole new set of people here who never knew Joe. Matt and Izzy as well as Danny. Life goes on. It just does. There isn't any other way.

But the mystery is still there. Why Joe made all those mistakes. Like Gramps said.

Did he do it on purpose? Is that possible?

It can't make any difference to him now. But I really, really want to understand what happened that night. To find the missing piece in the jigsaw.

There must be something I've forgotten, even though I've gone over and over it all, bit by bit, what happened last summer.

I look round the room, as if it might be hiding something. If only Joe had kept a notebook, like me, with all his feelings written down. Or written letters or something, *anything*, to show me what he was feeling like, last summer. There aren't even emails or texts or anything. Nothing left behind. No words at all.

So who might know? Who might he have talked to?

The answer is staring me in the face.

All the times I've come in here, and yet I've never noticed it before. I only see it now because I'm lying on Joe's bed, where he'd have lain, seeing as if through his eyes. Above the door frame there's a tiny photo propped up, like one you get from an instant photo booth at a station or somewhere.

Samphire.

Twenty-one

That night I dream about Huw. He's holding this girl in his arms, and of course it's Samphire, her long hair spilling over his tanned arm, but as I watch, she changes and becomes Izzy. He's holding Izzy, bending over her, kissing her open mouth. I want to call out a warning to her, but my voice is frozen over and I'm helpless, speechless, and then someone's pulling me away from the window. It's Matt, and I'm filled with longing for him to hold me like Huw's holding Izzy, and that's the moment I wake up, hot and thirsty in the early hours when it's still dark.

My heart's pounding. I push back the covers and lean out to the window, push it open a bit wider. In the stillness of a windless night the sea's voice calls loud and insistent, repeating itself, relentlessly pounding the shore.

Someone else is awake: I hear Evie and Gramps' door open; feet pad along the landing and down to the kitchen. The back door squeaks as it's pushed open. I can't see the back garden from here, but I imagine Evie standing on the lawn in bare feet, looking up at the stars. I hear the kitchen tap being turned on, and then footsteps back up the stairs, along the landing. The door shuts again.

Cooler now, I turn on my side and let the sound of the sea lull me back towards sleep. Just as I'm dropping off, it comes to me as a revelation, what I need to do next. It's obvious, really.

Talk to Huw. Ask him about Samphire. Find her. Track her down.

119

Do I dare?

*   *   *

I try not to think about it, the next few days. I decide I'm just going to be on holiday like everyone else. So on Thursday I go with the kids from the campsite on the boat trip to Bryluen. It's the best place to snorkel, in the calm water of the east bay, and this will be Danny's first go. I'm going to teach him.

I show him how to clear the mask and blow water out of the tube, and how to go backwards with the fins.

'You shouldn't really hold your breath for more than a few seconds,' I say.

He gets the hang of it quite fast, and we swim together, parallel to the shore. Maddie and Lisa and the others don't stay in long: it's freezing cold even with wetsuits. But I don't want to stop swimming. I love the way the light filters through the water and makes patterns on the wave-ridged sand. A shoal of tiny silver fish dart in front of us: we reach out our hands and the shoal parts like liquid mercury.

Danny stands up, spluttering. 'Had enough!'

I leave him behind and swim out deeper by myself. Spider crabs scuttle along near the deep shadow of rocks under a fringe of waving red sea-anenomes. I love the feel of my hair streaming out behind me and the speed with which I can glide below the surface with just a flick of the fins. And then the pressure in my lungs begins to build and I've got to breathe so I arch my back and fin gently up towards the sun. As I reach the surface I pull off the mask and take a huge shuddering breath.

I swim slowly back to Danny.

'Wow!' he says.

'I love it. I'd forgotten how much!'

'You stayed under ages.'

'You can survive longer without oxygen underwater than on dry land, you know.' I can practically hear Joe's voice telling me all this. *Your heart-rate slows and most of your blood goes to the brain, rather than the feet and hands. Oxygen-saving mode. Even if you're unconscious. But never ignore the desire to breathe. That's how people drown.*

Joe *knew* all this. Like he knew about boats, and currents, and navigation. My question about the accident won't go away; it's gnawing away at me, the invisible maggot at the core of a windfall apple. *He knew all this, and he still let it happen. Why?*

Maddie and Lisa wave from the beach. They're already dressed, making their way towards the café.

'Come on, then, show-off! Hurry up!' Danny says, teeth chattering. 'I'm totally freezing.'

*   *   *

Bryluen is bigger and busier than St Ailla. It has hotels and pubs and its own campsite and a sailing school, and at least five shops. You might think it'd be a relief to get off our tiny island and go somewhere else where there's more to do, but it's not like that for me at all. I feel unsettled all the time we're there. Even though I love the snorkelling, and it's fun larking about on the wide sandy beach with everyone, and watching Will and Ben try windsurfing, a bit of me can't help longing for it to be five o'clock so we can go and wait on the jetty for the *Spirit* to pick us up and take us home to our own island.

The first thing I notice as the boat comes round into the bay is that instead of Matt, it's Huw crewing and doing the tickets, just like he did last summer. My heart gives a lurch. It's as if I'm not being allowed to *forget*. Not that I can talk to Huw right now, of course. He's at work. There are too many people. But even so, I'm going to have to do it sooner or later.

'Where's Matt?' Lisa asks Huw as we climb on board.

'Getting things ready for tonight,' Huw says.

'Why? What's happening tonight?'

'Izzy's having a party,' he says. 'On the beach. You're all invited, of course.'

*   *   *

The boat's packed with day trippers. We stand together at the front of the boat, and even after the last load of holidaymakers have got off at Main Island and we're the only passengers left on board, we stay there, rather than sitting on the empty benches. As we come out of the sheltered harbour into the Sound, Dave revs up the engine. Huw and the others egg him on. Going against the current, the boat makes a huge wash that sprays over the bows and over us. Everyone laughs. We're wet through by the time we're back at St Ailla.

'Don't forget tonight,' Huw announces as we pile off again at our jetty. 'Eight o'clock on the beach.'

*   *   *

All the time I'm getting ready to go out, I'm working out what to say to Huw. He's bound to be there. It's a golden opportunity. But it's scary. For a start, I've hardly said two words to him this summer: I've been avoiding him as much as possible. I'm still too angry. Then there's the way he is—older, arrogant, a bit aloof—and that's all before actually thinking what to say, and how to begin.

You remember that girl last year? Samphire. Did you keep in touch? Have you got her address?

It sounds too weird.

Remember that girl last year? Did you know how much Joe liked her?

Weirder still.

I've been trying to work out something about my brother Joe . . .

Evie looks up from her paper as I come into the kitchen. 'That blue top suits you,' she says. 'Better than all those dark colours you've been wearing.'

'They're just my normal clothes,' I say. 'Everyone wears black, Evie.'

'Well. Enjoy the party. Take something warm for later. I won't wait up. Just put your head round the door so I know you're safely back.'

Smoke's already curling up from a huge driftwood fire by the time I get there, and Luke's playing his guitar. Izzy waves as I pick my way across the stones. She looks gorgeous: she's wearing this thin, floaty orange top and a long pink cotton skirt, like a sari. Her hair's loose down her back, straighter than usual. Matt stacks more wood on the fire and it sends a shower of sparks spiralling upwards. From the other side of the fire,

Maddie waves her can at me as a greeting. Lisa squeezes herself between Maddie and Huw. I can't see Danny anywhere. My courage is already draining away.

Maddie leans over towards me. 'Have you heard? Izzy's going away.'

'Back to her mum's,' Lisa adds.

'Why? How long for?'

'A level results. And her mum's birthday or something.' They both laugh.

I don't see anything funny about it.

'So Matt will be at a loose end,' Maddie says.

'We'll have to keep an eye on him,' Lisa says. 'Keep him busy. While the cat's away . . .'

It's horrible. I don't know what to think. Are they teasing me? Have they noticed something about Matt and me? Is it obvious to everyone?

It's a relief to see Danny and Hattie coming over.

Hattie gives me a hug.

'You've made a friend for life,' Danny says. 'Reading all those stories to her that afternoon.'

'I should hope so!' I smile gratefully at Hattie and she wriggles closer. 'So how come you're allowed to a party this late?'

'It's only for a while,' Danny says. 'Dad's taking her back in half an hour.'

We watch the fire together, and eat sausages and crisps. I try not to think about Maddie and Lisa, that *look*. I don't want to think about Izzy going away. Just as I'm getting to know her. Just when I need her.

Hattie gets hauled off by her dad soon after, kicking and going on. He lifts her on to his shoulders.

'I don't WANT to go to bed. It's not fair! I'm

124

NOT tired!'

I listen to their voices as they jog away across the beach, his jollying her along, playing at horses, her protesting all the way. A memory tugs at me. Riding like that on my dad's shoulders, and Joe running behind, trying to catch us, and much further behind, Mum, though I can't remember her really. I just know that's where she'd have been: not quite part of the game, and carrying all the beach stuff, probably. Somebody has to, after all. A sudden pang of loneliness grips me. Mum. Dad. Joe. Me. None of us together now.

The mood of the party changes once the families and young kids have gone. The fire looks brighter against a darkening sky. Matt and Izzy pile another load of driftwood on to the flames. Huw gets up to help them. It's not a random load of wood, I see now: it's the remains of an old boat, still nailed together at the bows. Odd, and sad, to see a boat burning.

'Like a funeral pyre,' Izzy says, as if she's read my thoughts. 'A Viking burial.'

'We should sail it out on to the sea still burning,' someone suggests, but no one moves. More cans and bottles are passed round. Danny hands me a bottle of beer.

'No thanks.'

'How was the snorkelling?' Izzy asks Danny.

'Cool.'

'I hear Freya's a bit of an expert,' Izzy says.

'She swims like a fish,' Danny says.

I don't say anything.

'That's because she's a water sign,' Izzy says. 'What about you?'

Danny hasn't a clue what she's talking about.

'When's your birthday?' I prompt.

'April.'

'So you're Aries, or Taurus. Fire, or Earth. Not water, anyway.'

'*What*?'

'Star signs,' I explain. 'Duh!'

'That's just stupid,' Danny says. 'How can stars possibly affect people?'

Izzy gets her dreamy look. 'There's more to life than we can know or understand, Danny boy. Not everything can be explained by science.'

'No?'

Izzy laughs. 'There you go: such a rationalist. You can't help it. You must be Taurus.'

Danny snorts and shoves Izzy so she crumples up, giggling, on to the pebbles.

'You don't really believe that stuff, do you?' Danny asks me, once Izzy's out of earshot.

'No, of course not. It's just fun, sometimes. And Izzy's right that we don't know everything. Not yet, anyway.' It's on the tip of my tongue to tell him about seeing Joe. But I hold back. 'Did you hear about Izzy going away?' I say instead.

'Yes. Huw's helping out instead, at the farm. It's only for a week. Don't look so miserable!'

'Who's miserable?' Izzy says, coming back over. 'I thought we'd cured you, Freya?'

'She doesn't want you to go away. She's missing you already,' Danny teases.

My cheeks burn.

Izzy hugs me. 'I'll miss you too. But it's not for long.'

Close up, her face is the shape of a heart. Her eyes are green like river water. She glances over to Maddie, Lisa and Huw.

'You can look after Matt for me,' she says quietly, so only I can hear. And then she goes over to join the others, and squeezes herself in between Huw and Matt. Matt puts his arm round her; she leans her head into the hollow of his neck.

I turn back to the fire. A sudden swirl of smoke makes my eyes water.

Look after Matt. Why did she say that?

Sparks from the burning boat explode into the sky. It's turned indigo now, a velvet cloak studded with hundreds and thousands of stars. So many tiny stars, that with my watery eyes I can hardly tell which is fire-spark and which is real star. I'm not crying exactly, but the tears keep coming. I'm not even sad, this minute: I love sitting round the fire like this; I've actually started to feel like I belong here again, with everyone else. Luke playing the guitar; voices rising and falling . . .

'You staying late?'

Danny's voice makes me jump. 'I don't know!'

He looks hurt.

'I'm just enjoying being here,' I say more kindly. 'Not thinking, for once.' But of course, soon as I say that I've started up again. Huw. Izzy. The rest.

'Who's for a swim?' someone shouts.

It's a ritual, the midnight swim. A load of them are already stripping off down to their shorts, laughing and joking. Matt looks at Izzy but she shakes her head.

He goes ahead anyway, without her, pulling off his shirt and hobbling barefoot down the shingle after the others. Lisa and Maddie paddle in the shallows, jeans rolled up, whooping encouragement.

'Is it safe, in the dark?' Danny asks.

'They won't stay in long. They're all together. It's fine,' Izzy says.

Danny looks torn; as if he half wants to join in, half doesn't. Izzy comes to his rescue. 'Put some more wood on the fire for us, Danny.'

Laughter, splashing, shouts drift up the beach from the dark water. I watch the sky for shooting stars.

'It's really late,' Danny says. 'Think I'll be going back. You coming, Freya?'

'Not yet.'

'See ya, then.'

'Bye, Danny.'

Izzy and I watch him go. Then we lie down again, side by side, under the cloak of stars. She squeezes my hand, 'Oh Danny boy,' she says wistfully.

'What?'

'Just a song. My nana used to sing it.'

We're quiet together. I close my eyes.

'He does like you, though,' she says, after a while. 'Doesn't he?'

I think of Matt, and what she said before. Perhaps it was just a joke. She didn't mean anything by it.

I stay there with my eyes shut. I hear and feel the people coming out of the water, back up the beach, as a kind of vibration in the ground beneath me.

'Urgh! You're dripping all over me!' Izzy's voice.

Matt's leaning over her. I imagine their kiss: his cold salty lips on her warm ones. I listen as people dry themselves and get dressed and rake up the fire to get more warmth out of it. Luke plays some wild flamenco stuff on the guitar. Izzy stretches and sits up. 'Dancing time,' she says.

I lie still, listening, getting sleepier and sleepier. The air's still warm, even away from the fire, as if the pebbles store heat from the day. Voices and music and laughter spin in my head, and weaving in and out and under it all is the voice of the sea, shushing and soothing me, steady like breathing.

*   *   *

'Where's Freya?'

'She went back ages ago.'

'No she didn't. She's sleeping over there.'

Boots crunch over pebbles. I feel someone close up. A cool hand smoothes a strand of hair back from my forehead.

'Freya?' Matt's voice.

I open my eyes.

He's kneeling next to me. 'Time to go back. You've been asleep!'

'What time is it?'

'No idea. But you can't stay here. We're all going back now. We're the last ones.'

The fire's burned almost to ash. Matt and Izzy kick shingle to quench the last glowing embers. Izzy gathers up the remaining bottles and cans. I walk back with them, stumbling along the path to the campsite still half-asleep. Matt takes the box of bottles and rubbish so Izzy can hold my arm and keep me upright.

The campsite looks different at this hour. The tents are patches of darkness against dark grass. One dim light on the wall of the shower barn casts huge shadows over the field. You can sense all the sleeping, silent people, almost hear them breathing.

At Izzy's tent, Matt puts down the box. The clanking of empty bottles sounds eerily loud. So does the sound of the tent being unzipped.

'Can you walk Freya back home?' Izzy whispers to Matt. 'I'm absolutely shattered.'

I feel his hand on my arm. Nothing seems real. I'm sleepwalking.

'Sleep tight,' Izzy whispers after me. 'See you in a week or so, Freya. Be happy, remember!'

I've chilled right down, but Matt's body is warm next to mine. My arms and legs are stiff and achy. We're going under the trees, up the lane. We pass the farmhouse in silence. Not even the dogs are awake. Now we're at the gate.

'All right now?' Matt says. 'Or shall I take you right in? You're asleep on your feet!'

'I'm OK. Thanks for bringing me back.'

He steers me through the gate. 'Night, then.' He touches my hand, and as I turn he pulls me very slightly towards him. For one moment I think he's going to kiss me. But he doesn't. He just squeezes my hand, and lets me go.

Twenty-two

'Izzy left this,' Evie says as I come down into the kitchen the next morning. She points to a large carrier bag on the kitchen table.

Izzy's gone. My stomach lurches as I remember.

'What is it?'

'She left you a note. It was early. She didn't want me to wake you.'

130

Thought you might like these. I'll be getting new stuff off Mum. If you don't want them/ they don't fit just throw them out or give to someone else/recycle or whatever. Be happy. (Wear the necklace!) Take care of Matt for me. See you soon. Love Izzy xx

I pull out an armful of soft blue fabric, shake it out: it's a skirt, made of fine Indian cotton. I hold it against me.

'Pretty!' Evie says. 'It could do with an iron.'

'It's meant to be crinkly like that.'

There's a green silk top, and two dresses. The bright colours glow in the dark kitchen.

'They're just right for this hot weather,' Evie says. 'You don't want to be in jeans all the time.'

Up in my room, I try them on. I don't feel like me: I never wear dresses. Or bright colours like red, or orange. I don't look like me, either. I look like someone new, or perhaps just a different version of me. In the end I leave the blue skirt on and take my breakfast out into the garden, where Gramps is sitting in a deckchair.

He tries to do a wolf whistle when he sees me. 'Going dancing?' he says. 'Can I come? Give us a twirl!'

I laugh and spin round so the skirt floats out. 'You're better, then?'

'Much.'

I make us tea, and Evie comes out to sit with Gramps too, in the shade of the apple tree.

'What are you going to do today?' she asks.

'Not sure. I'll see what everyone at the campsite's doing.'

'Danny?'

'And the others.'

But it's Huw I actually go looking for. My palms are sweating already, from me just thinking about talking to him, but I can't put it off any longer.

*　　　*　　　*

I find him down on the jetty, helping Dave load boxes and crates on to the supplies boat. I watch him. It takes ages. I go and sit on the bit of wall, like we all did last summer when we waited for the new arrivals. After a while Huw notices me; he sort of half nods in my direction. When he's loaded the last crate he strolls over.

'All right?' he asks. He takes a packet of papers and a tin of tobacco from his pocket and starts rolling himself a cigarette. He leans against the wall. He cups his hand round the roll-up so he can light it with a match.

'Yep.' I swing my legs, just like some silly schoolkid. Then I get a grip.

'Can I ask you something?'

He stays staring ahead, down the jetty. The supplies boat has cast its mooring rope; the engine revs and a cloud of dark smoke follows in its wake. 'Well?'

My heart's pounding so fast I'm surprised he can't hear it. Maybe he can.

'It's about last summer.'

He takes another drag of the cigarette. He turns and looks at me; he reaches his hand out and touches my shoulder. 'I know, Freya. It was a terrible thing.'

I have to keep staring straight ahead, otherwise

I'll dissolve completely. 'The thing is,' I start. 'The thing is . . .'

'What?'

'I've been thinking about it all over again . . .'

'Of course. Me too.'

That throws me off guard. But of course he has. Who wouldn't? I'm surprised he's come back to the island, even, after what happened.

'I've been trying to work some things out,' I say in a rush, before I lose my nerve completely. 'And I need to talk to that girl—Sam; find out what she remembers about Joe, and that night, before the accident.'

Huw frowns. He throws the cigarette down and crushes it under his boot.

I carry on, my voice sounding silly and high-pitched I'm so nervous. 'Do you know where I can find her? Her phone number or an address or something, I mean?'

'No,' he says. 'Why would I?'

My cheeks are burning up now. I don't know what to say.

Huw goes on. 'Joe was mad about her. Cra–zy! Poor bloke. 'Cos she wasn't bothered. Not after the novelty wore off. You don't want to talk to her, Freya. She can't tell you anything about your brother. It won't help.'

I'm so close to tears I don't even look up when I hear the engine of a boat slowing down as it approaches the jetty. Huw's hand is still on my shoulder, pressing down. 'He wasn't even with her that night, when the accident happened,' he says.

Something suddenly boils up inside me. It's the way he's talking so sort of casually about her and Joe. But I don't shout and rant. My voice comes

133

out ice cold.

'I know,' I say. 'But you were.'

Huw seems to go still.

'I saw you. You and Samphire were together in that house. You didn't care, or think what it might be like for Joe, did you?'

'Hey,' Huw says. 'Steady on, Freya!'

'You knew how much Joe liked her. You said just now, he was crazy about her. So what if he saw the two of you together? Imagine what he'd have felt like then!'

Huw shifts away from me. 'He was crazy to *like* her so much, I meant. She wasn't worth it. She just wanted a bit of fun. Amusing herself on her holidays. It didn't mean anything to her. Joe deserved better than that.'

We're both quiet, remembering.

Huw starts up again. 'I'm not proud of what I did—with her, I mean. I'm sorry if Joe was upset. Sam said it was over. She'd finished with him. Didn't care. Joe's *accident* wasn't anything to do with her, Freya. Or me.'

I stare at him. His shoulders are hunched up, his face stony. I wonder if he does feel guilty, really. But I can't hate him. He's saying the truth, as far as he knows it. He's three years older than Joe. He's probably had loads of girlfriends. He's good-looking. Even I can see why Sam would fancy him more than Joe. Sixteen-year-old, inexperienced, love-sick Joe.

I'm suddenly crumpling up, defeated. I wish I hadn't said anything now. It hasn't got me anywhere. I just look stupid.

'What's going on here?' a voice says. 'Freya?'

It's Matt. Out of nowhere. Then I remember that

134

boat. It must have been his.

I jump down from the wall. 'It's OK,' I say. 'We were just talking.'

'You look all upset.'

'I'm all right,' I say.

'I've got work to do,' Huw says. 'Sorry I couldn't help, Freya.'

'I've got to go anyway,' I say.

I start walking up the path, take the left fork towards the pub. Behind me, I hear Matt and Huw's voices, slightly raised, as if they're arguing about something.

Running footsteps behind me crunch the gravelly stones. I don't turn round.

Matt catches me up. He walks beside me for a while. I don't speak.

'Freya? What was going on, with Huw, just now?'

'Nothing.'

'Slow down a bit! Did he upset you?'

'It's nothing,' I say. 'I asked him a question. It was my fault.'

'About what? What do you mean?'

'Nothing. Please.'

'If you're sure . . .'

'Yes!'

'So where're you going now?'

'Home.'

'You're going the wrong way!'

'The *long* way home,' I say, and he smiles.

He doesn't turn back, like I'm expecting. He keeps on walking beside me. I slow down.

'Shouldn't you be at work?' I say, after a while.

'You sound just like Izzy!'

Izzy. She'll be miles away by now.

'Did you see her off, this morning?' I ask him.

135

'I did. I took her over to Main Island to get the early boat.'

In my mind's eye I see him kissing her goodbye, and watching the big ferry make its way out of the harbour at Main Island. He stands there till it's just a speck in the middle of the ocean. I realise, suddenly, that it actually makes me feel better, thinking about the way they love each other: that there are good things, as well as sad ones. People who care about each other, stay together, even if they sometimes do things apart. A bit like Evie and Gramps.

'Want to go for a swim with me later?' Matt asks.

'OK . . . If you're sure.'

'After I've done the afternoon ferry. Sixish?'

I nod.

'Sand bar? Or Beady Pool?'

'The sand bar's nicer for swimming,' I say. My voice sounds shaky. I'm trembling.

He turns back, I walk on, past the turning for the sand bar and Gara, on towards Beady Pool. I try to forget about my conversation with Huw about Samphire, so I can think properly about Matt asking me to swim with him. What it means.

Evie's Bronze Age well is near here: I wonder about stopping to find it, making a wish, but I haven't got anything to give in return; Izzy's blue skirt has no pockets, and I can't even find a pebble to drop down. There's a load of bracken and other ferns, and the soil is peaty and damp, rather than stony like it is on other places along the cliff. So I don't stop. What would I wish for, anyway?

I think of Matt and my heart gives a little leap.

I finger the talisman necklace Izzy made me. I wear it all the time now; I've got used to the feel of

136

the stone, cool against my skin in the hollow of my neck.

Izzy's good at giving things. She travels lightly and she gives things away, passes them on. Her own happiness is a kind of gift. Then there's the necklace, the bag of clothes. Those words on her note come into my mind again. *Take care of Matt . . .*

Is Matt a gift to me, too?

*　　　*　　　*

Danny's loitering in the lane, looking over the gate at the old lighthouse buildings. The *For Sale* notice is still up, though it's beginning to fade and blister in the sun.

'Hi,' he says. 'I just called for you. No one was in.'

'They were probably in the garden, at the back. Didn't hear you.'

'So where've you been?' Danny asks. 'You're all dressed up!'

'Not you as well!' I say. 'I put on Izzy's skirt and suddenly everyone's commenting! I must have looked a right scruff before.'

'No, I didn't mean that!' He's gone red.

'I know. Just teasing you. So what did you want? When you called?'

'Nothing, really. Just to see what you were doing today.' He picks off a poppy seed head and chucks it into the garden.

'I went to talk to Huw.'

'Oh?'

'About Sam.'

'And?'

137

'It was a disaster.'

'Why?'

'How he was . . . he didn't want to talk about her. Said he didn't have her number or anything.'

Danny still looks puzzled.

'I thought it might be another clue, you know? About Joe. If I could speak to her, she might tell me how Joe was feeling, or what he'd been talking about. Something. Anything.'

Danny looks doubtful.

He starts walking, and I go with him, past my house and towards the campsite. There's the usual queue for milk and stuff at the farmhouse back door. No Izzy, of course. Sally's dealing with everyone. She sees us and waves. 'Gig-racing tonight!' she calls. 'Don't forget! Boat leaving at seven, if you want to come.'

'What's that about?' Danny asks.

'Gig-racing? Oh, it's a kind of island thing, racing these boats called gigs. Like the ones they used to row out to pilot big ships. Each island has a team. Dave does a trip out on the *Spirit,* to watch. It's fun. You should go.'

'Will you?'

'I might. It's a good laugh. You have to sing and cheer and stuff. Some of the blokes strip down, put on warpaint. It's all very *tribal.* Afterwards everyone goes to the pub.'

A dog barks. The almost-grown pup comes hurtling round the corner and jumps up.

'Hello, Bess!' I pat her warm back. Her fur is still slightly woolly and soft, not silky smooth like Bonnie's.

'Hey, Freya! I've got a really good idea!' Danny says. 'How about asking Sally about that Sam girl?

138

She must keep details for the campsite. Phone numbers and emails and stuff. She could look up her books for last summer for you.'

'I'm not sure . . . Maybe Huw's right, and it won't help. Sam won't know anything. She might not even remember Joe.'

Danny looks stunned. 'How could she possibly forget? An accident like that . . .'

'She might not even have known about it. She left that Saturday morning, the day after.'

'Wasn't everyone talking about it? Surely it was a huge thing?'

'How do I know?' I say miserably. 'I wasn't at the campsite, was I? We were all in shock, up at the house. It wasn't general knowledge till later that morning, and she'd have left before then.'

The truth is, I don't know. It's all a blur. I hardly remember that day at all. Mum and Dad arrived by helicopter to Main Island, sometime in the morning.

Danny's still talking.

'What exactly did he say?' Danny asks again.

'Who?'

'Huw.'

'Not a lot. That Sam was just messing about. Having fun. Didn't care about Joe, really. That it was over, anyway, between her and Joe.'

Danny's quiet for a bit, deep in thought. 'How would he really know? Maybe he's wrong about that. It's worth a try, isn't it, finding Sam? Don't give up so easily.'

'It hurts too much,' I say. 'Sorry, Danny. I don't want to talk about it any more.'

We walk on. Bess trots beside me, as if she belongs to us. I keep my hand on her warm back.

At the gate to the field, she barks and turns and races back to the farmhouse.

Danny's family are sitting in the sun outside their tent, reading and drinking coffee. Hattie waves to me and runs over. My heart sinks a bit.

'We're going to another island today and there's palm trees,' she says. 'Are you coming? Please?'

I shake my head. 'Not today.'

'What about that boat thing, this evening?' Danny says.

'Probably.'

I turn back to the house, to wait for it to be six o'clock.

Twenty-three

'The doctor called again,' Evie tells me as I come in the back door. 'And I've just spoken to your dad.'

'What did he say?'

'He's worried about Gramps. Wants to see him. He's going to sort out his work, phone back later. He sends his love to you, Freya. Perhaps you'd speak to him this evening?'

I mull this over, up in my room. It sounds serious. Like, Evie thinks Gramps is really sick. But he didn't seem it this morning. He said he was getting better. He came downstairs and was sitting in the garden and everything. He's back in bed now, resting. I can't bear it if something happens to Gramps. I look in on him, but he's asleep. It's the new pills, Evie says, making him drowsy.

At five, I get my swimming stuff and notebook and set off for the sand bar, to wait there for Matt. I've been daydreaming about him all afternoon.

The sun's still hot. Early evening will be a good time for swimming, with the sea coming in over sun-warmed sand. I've got my swimming things on under my clothes, to make it easier to change. I find a sheltered place to sunbathe, up near the dunes at the Gara end of the beach, away from the day trippers who just plump down on the nearest bit of sand at the end of the path. I doodle in my notebook, to pass the time.

I've almost given up on Matt when I see a figure making its way along the sand. I can't see his face at first, but I recognise the way he walks. My heartbeat quickens even though I'm trying to stay cool. *Think of Izzy*, I keep reminding myself. My legs suddenly look too pale; I cover them up with the blue skirt and pretend to be busy drawing.

His shadow falls across the white page.

'Freya. Hi. Ready for a swim, then?'

I nod self-consciously.

'I'm so hot! I've been looking forward to this for hours!' He strips off his T-shirt and drops it and his towel in a pile next to my stuff. He grins. 'I hear you swim like a fish.'

'Says who?'

'Izzy; Danny.'

'Well then!'

Matt laughs. 'I know. Have you seen Izzy swim?'

I realise with surprise that I haven't. All those times we've been on the beach together, she's never actually gone into the water.

141

'Race you!' He starts running, and I join him. He's much faster than me, but I do my best, and I manage to dive in straight away, rather than my usual slow wade out, and once we're in I'm easily as strong a swimmer as he is: stronger, even. He can swim fast for a short while but can't keep going like I can.

The water's freezing on my sun-heated body, but it's exhilarating. *Waterbaby*, Mum used to call me. I get into a steady rhythm, my breathing deep and regular. There are only the smallest waves: the wind's dropped for once. I could go on and on for ever, further and further out. The water gets deep very quickly off the bar, but it's crystal clear, so you can see right down to the wave-ridged sand beneath. I turn on to my back to float. Above me the sky is blue blue blue, fading at the edges to white.

Matt's treading water, beckoning me back. I flip over, swim slow overarm strokes towards him.

'OK, you win!' He grins, and shakes his wet hair out of his beautiful tanned face. 'Don't go out any further. The tide's coming in and the currents start to pull you out.'

'I know,' I say. 'I've swum here every summer since I was little.'

'I can't stay long,' Matt says. 'I said I'd row in the gig race tonight. They're one man down.'

'Have you done it before?'

'Not here, but back home, yes. Don't look so worried! I'm not that bad at it!'

'Race you back to the beach?' I do my best crawl, and just to show off, when I see how far ahead I am, butterfly. The sea seems unnaturally still, as if it's holding its breath.

I walk up the beach to get my towel, turn to watch Matt stride out of the sea. He shakes himself like a wet dog. His wet shorts cling to his body.

'Here!' I hand him his towel.

'Thanks. That's better.' He rubs his head and his chest. He turns to me. 'You're still dripping wet! Come here!' He leans over and wipes the water from my face with his towel. He's so close I feel his breath warm on my cheek.

Does he have any idea what he's doing to me? I'm like melted butter. My head's all muzzy. But he seems oblivious to the effect he has.

'Any idea of the time?'

I reach down for my watch. *Joe's* watch. 'Twenty to seven.'

'Just time to phone Izzy before I get going. Should be helping down at the boathouse. Do you want to come?'

I shake my head. I can't speak for a minute.

He chatters on. 'Thanks for the swim. You *do* swim like a fish. Izzy was right.'

He has his back to me now. He's fished his phone from his pocket and he's dialling her number. I see him smile as she picks up. I lie down on the warm sand, on my tummy, so he can't see my face. Not that he's looking.

I pull myself together. What else did I expect? What would I have thought, really, if he'd done anything else? He belongs to Izzy and Izzy belongs to him. It's so stupid, feeling like this. He's just being friendly. There are different kinds of touch. I shouldn't take everything so . . . literally. But it's like my head knows one thing, and my body feels another. They don't quite match up.

143

Once Matt's gone, I get dry and dressed and start walking back. I pass the pub and glimpse the team, down below at the boathouse slipway, getting the gig ready. Six blokes: Luke, Ben's dad and uncle, two of Dave's mates, whose names I don't know, plus Matt. Over at the jetty Dave's steering the *Spirit* round to pick up a queue of people. Perhaps I should go, after all?

I hesitate, at the top of the track, dithering over what to do. Danny turns up just at that moment. 'Good!' he says, when he sees me.

'I'm on my way back,' I tell him. 'Not coming on the boat.'

His face falls. 'Oh well,' he says. 'I guess you've been a million times before.'

'Yes.'

'They're doing the long race, right out to the Bird islands and back to Main Island.'

'The triangle.'

Danny fishes around in his pocket and pulls out a scrap of torn paper. He hands it to me rather sheepishly. 'I got this for you.'

I turn it over. Numbers, handwritten. 'What is it?'

'Her phone number. That girl, Samphire. Her mother's phone, anyway.'

'Danny! How come?'

'I saw Sally. I asked her. I was right, see? She did have it.'

'What did you say?'

'Just that you wanted to get in touch with a girl who was here last year. She wasn't bothered. Well,

144

she was a bit busy at the time, but I said it was important.'

'Oh, Danny!'

'What? Was it wrong?'

'I don't know . . .'

The ship bell rings. Dave revs the boat engine. People have started boarding. 'Sure you won't come?' Danny asks.

I shake my head. 'But thanks for the number.'

*   *   *

Do I really mean that?

I'm touched that Danny got it for me. Really. He's quite shy; it would have been a big effort: finding Sally, asking, all that. I stare at the paper in my hand. Now it's a reality, I don't know what to do. I could actually phone. Leave a message. Speak to Sam, even. I finger the numbers, carefully written in Danny's hand in black ink on the scrap of lined paper.

Shouts and whoops echo out over the Sound. The race hasn't started yet, but all the gigs from the off-islands are making their way to the starting buoy, followed by the flotilla of supporting boats. I almost wish I'd gone after all.

I dump my wet towel and swimsuit on the draining board in the kitchen. Evie's talking on the phone in the front room. She waves at me through the open door.

'It's your dad! Don't go anywhere!'

I sit on the arm of the sofa.

Evie's nodding and looking pleased. 'Goodbye, Martin,' she says, and hands the phone to me.

'Hi, Dad.'

It's weird hearing his voice, so close and clear in my ear. He sounds fine. He says he's missing me.

'What's the house like?' I ask.

'Not bad, for a rented place. It'll do for now. Your mum's still looking for somewhere else, though.'

Panic grips my belly. 'What do you mean?'

'For us to buy,' Dad says.

I let out my breath. For a moment I'd thought he meant just Mum, a house by herself . . .

'There's one here for sale,' I blurt out. 'The one attached to the old lighthouse.' I don't even know I'm going to say that until the words come bleating out of my mouth.

'Oh, Freya!' Dad says, after a bit of a silence. 'Not practical, I'm afraid.'

'It'd be a great project,' I say. 'Doing it up and everything. Imagine.'

Why am I saying this? It's totally crazy.

The architect bit of Dad comes to the fore. I know he *is* imagining, just for a brief moment, what a great time he'd have designing something round the actual lighthouse. 'You're right,' he says. 'But no. Your mum wouldn't ever contemplate living there. You know that, Freya.'

I do. For her it would be a constant reminder of losing Joe. Rubbing salt in wounds: the cruel sea, always there, less than a mile away in all directions. Then there's the fact there's no proper shops. No work. Hardly any neighbours. And being right next door, practically, to Dad's parents, lovely as they are. . . she wouldn't want that either. Plus it's hundreds of miles away from her friends, of course, and from my school . . . and in winter you get stranded for days. OK, a million good reasons

146

why not.

'Well,' I say, changing the subject. 'Are you and Mum coming over?'

'For the Bank Holiday weekend. *I* am, anyway. Your mother doesn't think she's ready yet.'

'Is she there? Can I talk to her?'

'Not right now. Not a good time, love. Tomorrow, maybe.'

I give up. I put the phone down. I think about Mum, ghostly thin, still grieving. She doesn't even want to speak to me, now.

*   *   *

I wish Evie hadn't made me speak to Dad. It's stirred everything up again. But maybe because of that, I get Danny's scrap of paper out again and without letting myself stop to change my mind I just dial the number.

Evie's clattering around in the kitchen. I kick the door to while the phone rings and rings. It's a landline, not a mobile. No one answers. I'm just about to put the phone down again when a voicemail clicks on. It's one of those automatic reply services, not a personal message. *The person you called is not available . . . please leave a message after the tone.*

I clear my throat, then start talking. 'This is a message for Samphire,' I say. 'From Freya, Joe's sister, from last summer, remember? Can you call me? I'd like to talk to you . . . about Joe.' I leave my mobile number.

My hand shakes as I replace the handset. I'm shivering all over. It's in her hands now. All I have to do is wait.

Only later, lying on Joe's bed, do I start to wonder what exactly I've gone and done.

Maybe it wasn't even the right number. They could easily have moved. Wasn't Sam talking about that, even, last summer?

She probably won't phone back. Why would she?

If she knows about Joe, why would she?

And if she doesn't? No reason. She won't phone.

What if she does phone, and she doesn't know about the accident, and I have to tell her about everything? Imagine that.

What good will any of it do, now?

Have I just made another stupid mistake, Joe?

If only he'd answer.

His room seems emptier than ever. Nothing's ever moved in here, except when Evie cleans. His books, CDs, the shells and things, all lie untouched. The edges of the posters on the walls are beginning to curl. He'd have moved on from them by now, if he were still here. He'd have new pictures. You can't keep everything the same. You shouldn't want to.

Samphire's unsmiling face stares coldly down from the small photo over the door. I can't stand seeing it any longer. I pull a chair over, stand on it so I can reach to take it down. It's dusty, slightly yellow at the edges. I turn it over.

Scribbled on the back are two words and a date, in Joe's handwriting.

First time 18 August

First time for what? But I know really. I'm not that stupid.

It's horrible. It's like reading someone's diary when you absolutely know you shouldn't. I've gone too far, prying into his secret life, into places which

148

are nothing to do with me. Suddenly and absolutely, as good as if he's saying it out loud, for real, I hear Joe's older-brother voice in my head: *Piss off, Freya. Get your own life.*

Hands shaking, I tear the photo into tiny pieces. It's still not enough; I want to destroy the evidence completely. I shove the fragments into the fireplace and light them with a match from the box on Joe's shelf. A small flame licks along the torn edges. I watch the flame flare up and then die until there's just a tiny pile of ash-flakes in the hearth. It only takes seconds. I open the window wide to let out the stink.

The air outside is heavy and still. The scent of full-blown roses and something sour and disgusting, like rotting vegetation, rises from the flower bed beneath the window.

I'm sick of me.

I'm sick of all this searching and trying to work things out.

I straighten the bedspread, put the chair back in its place, check the fire's completely out, and go into my own room. I lie on the bed, don't turn the light on. The room gets darker, still I don't move. Evie knocks on the door, to see if I'm all right, and I call out *yes, just having an early night,* so she leaves me alone after that. I don't undress. I check my phone: no messages. I leave it switched on.

It's hot and stuffy even at this hour. I open the window wider, to get some air. My notebook's lying on the table: I pick it up and start leafing back through the pages I've written this summer, re-reading everything, looking at the doodles and sketches, retracing my steps. This summer. Last summer.

I stare at the drawing of the maze I did a while back. It's like a picture of my own mind: the way I go back and round, searching for a way through, taking wrong turnings and finding dead ends. All this searching, to find a way into the centre, to find out the truth of what really happened to Joe.

You could stop all that, I tell myself. It doesn't have to be this way. The simple truth is this: Joe died. I miss him so bad it's like a physical pain running through my whole body, like mineral through rock. But I can't change any of that. And maybe I'll never know, for real, what actually happened, and why. Maybe there are some things I can't know, and that's what I have to accept.

*　　　*　　　*

Right now, all I want to do is to clear the muddle out of my head, wash it away.

Wash it away.

Water. Cool and deep and dark and inviting.

Swimming.

The way it feels to swim, my arms and legs strong, driving me forward, and the water running over my head.

How simple everything is, reduced to that. One arm, and the other. Legs kicking. Moving forward. Free.

My heart's beating fast, my stomach fluttering. It's all I want to do now: swim. Even this late, in the dark, in the cold sea. Overwhelming, the need for it.

Evie's with Gramps in their room. I don't want

her worrying about me as well, so I creep past their door, down the stairs, take my towel and my damp swimsuit from the rail in the bathroom, and slip out of the back door without her hearing.

The air outside is cooler than I expected. I hesitate, then open the shed door and take Joe's old wetsuit from the hook. Its weight over my arm makes me feel safe, as if Joe himself is close by.

It's not completely dark yet. Away from the lights of the house I can see well enough, once my eyes adjust. The sky is clear, a moon rising. The sea will be too high at the sand bar for safe swimming, so I aim for Beady Pool instead. As I come over the brow of the hill at the centre of the island I glimpse the lights from the pub; voices and laughter drift over in waves on the wind. I imagine everyone from the gig race, drinking and chatting outside. Matt. Danny.

The lane is deserted. No one sees me make my way down the path to the beach. The rising moon weaves a silvery path over the dark water, catching the tips of the waves limping in on to the sand between dark rocks. I don't stop to think about what I'm doing. I pull on the wetsuit—too big, but not as much as I expected, not enough to matter— and walk straight out into the waves, flinching as the cold water seeps in next to my skin. As soon as I'm deep enough I start to swim.

Twenty-four

Swimming at night is completely different from swimming in the light, in the daytime. The rocks either side of the beach loom blacker and bigger. It's harder to judge distances. The voice of the sea is louder, wilder, slapping against the rocks, scouring the shore. The water itself seems smooth, thicker than in the day, as if it's extra buoyant. I change stroke to front crawl.

Each long stroke takes me out further, till I'm beyond the rocks and can make out the dark line of the whole bay, right across to the black gap which is where the sand bar would be if the tide was lower. A slight frisson of fear ripples along my vertebrae; for the first time it feels slightly dangerous, being out alone on the water, at night. Every so often the sound of voices—singing— comes across the water from the pub. It's not so very far away. But no one knows I'm here. If I called out, no one would hear.

I stop swimming, turn on to my back, float. Bobbing on the black sea under this huge starry sky, I start to feel calm, lulled and soothed by the water that holds and surrounds me. Everything else drops away. Nothing matters. Sam, Huw, all that complicated stuff seems trivial and unnecessary. I give myself up to the water, float with my arms stretched out. But it won't let me stay still; now I've stopped swimming I can feel the pull and tug of the current drawing me out.

My body temperature is stable now, insulated by Joe's wetsuit. I flip over and start swimming again.

The movement wakes me up: energy fizzes along every nerve and muscle in my body. I keep my breathing steady: in, out, long breaths that take the air deep inside, a flow along my blood. It seems completely right, swimming here by myself. The water, deep and clean and cold, washes through my mind, cleansing me of thought, until that's all there is: water. Clear and open and free.

With each forward pull of my arms I dip my face down, turn my head sideways, breathe, dip again. Steady, easy, regular strokes. Time doesn't mean anything any more. I can't tell if I've been swimming for ten minutes or an hour. I don't care.

I lift my head again, to check where I am. Water runs over my skull, down my face. My hair's plastered to my cheek, suddenly stinging with cold. I've had my eyes shut, and now they're open I see how dark it's become. The moon seems to have disappeared. My teeth are chattering: it's time to go back. My night swim has done exactly what I wanted. I feel strong and free and empty at last. No thoughts. Just me, here, now, swimming.

My eyes search for bearings. I can't tell for a moment where the line of land goes, or how far it is back to the beach. This side of the island you can't see the sweep of the lighthouse beam, just layer upon layer of darkness. For a second I wonder if I've somehow swum right out, past the end of the island altogether, and my belly tightens. Then the moon comes out from behind an edge of cloud, and I recognise a line of rock, blacker against the sky, where wind and rain have sculpted the rock into contorted shapes like gargoyles. The tide and the current have taken me way off course. I can just about make out where the beach should

153

be, at Beady Pool. I start to swim back in that direction.

The tide must have turned. Ebbing, it's pulling away from the beach, so I'm having to swim against it. My arms and legs begin to ache. The dull needling in my stomach starts again; not pain, exactly, more like hunger, or fear. I mustn't get cramp now. I can't afford to float, to stop swimming, because the strong ebb tide will carry on, sweeping me out, relentlessly.

My breathing starts to become raggedy. I lose the rhythm and take a wrong breath, gulp water instead of air. The pain shoots deep into my lungs.

Just keep going. Steady. You're strong. You can do this. It's fine. Just water, and waves.

I try breaststroke: the different movement gives my arms a rest, but it's not strong enough to take me forward. The tide is more powerful than me. I don't seem to be getting any closer to the beach. Cold seeps into my flesh, my bones. My legs hurt. My chest aches.

A wave goes over my head just as I'm taking in a huge breath, and salt water fills my mouth. I spit it out; flail, panicking.

My mind's suddenly in overdrive.

This is how it happens: one minute you're in control. Then not.

The sea is not cruel, like Mum said, or even indifferent. It's just sea, governed by the laws of nature: it doesn't have feelings at all. The moon pulls the tides: the current sweeps out towards the open sea.

*   *   *

You're cold and you're tired, and you can't swim much longer. The wind gets up, the waves get bigger. You're drifting, the waves swamp you, carry you out further and further towards the line of jagged rocks at the end of the island, and there's nothing you can do, not any longer. You haven't the breath, the energy's sapped right out of you. So it goes on, and you're weaker and more exhausted.

You don't care any more. You're drifting, flotsam, with no will of your own. You feel sleepy. You feel nothing. The water carries you out, on and on, until a bigger wave catches you, lifts your body, sweeps it forward, breaks and smashes you down on to the rocks. Your skull cracks.

It's just an accident. You never meant it to happen like this. All you wanted was to get your head clear, sort yourself out, and start all over again, nothing more complicated than that. Swimming, sailing, whatever: horses for courses . . . You never meant to die. Of course not.

*　　　*　　　*

Another wave. Another gulp of water. Salt.

Freezing cold.

Numb.

Can't struggle.

Can't.

That early morning on Periglis, years ago, when we found the body of the drowned fisher-boy: remember, Joe? Peaceful. Nothing hurting any more.

'Full fathom five thy father lies;
Of his bones are coral made . . .'

155

Gramps.

Your precious life
Be happy
We love you to bits
Take care, Freya!

Numb now. Sleepy. Drifting.
  It doesn't matter, not any more.
  Nothing matters.
  Joe's face is pale, like the moon's reflection in the dark water. He gasps for air; I feel his breath, close up to my ear.
  The next shuddering breath is mine. Hands hold me, lift me up, so that with my next breath I get air, not water. My brother is swimming beside me, holding me up with one arm so I can rest and breathe again, steadily piloting me towards the shore.
  Minutes, hours.
  I'm hardly swimming at all, but Joe is, steady at my side. He won't let me give up. He carries me in, closer to the beach. It's just enough to let me rest, just long enough for me to get my breath back. My arms and legs start to tingle, energy seeping back in. I begin swimming, sidestroke, again.
  My arm, reaching out, scoops through the water.
  Kick legs.
  Dip. Scoop, pull through the water.
  Breathe deep, steady. Find the rhythm again.
  Joe's arm is still beneath me, supporting, but I can hardly feel it now.
  Almost there.
  Next time I lift my head I can see breaking surf,

the slope of the beach. We're swimming in shallow water. Finally, my feet find the sandy bottom.

Finally, Joe lets me go.

*   *   *

I don't look back. By the time I've staggered up the beach to my towel and clothes he's gone. I'm shaking all over, cold to the core, sick. But I'm safe.

The wetsuit clings to my trembling, freezing body: I've hardly the strength to peel it off and dry my goose-pimpled flesh, or pull on my clothes. Bit by bit, teeth chattering, I manage it, and the blood begins to flow again, tingling and warm, all through my body. As I start the walk back, it gets stronger, like a warm flow from the top of my wet scalp to the tips of my fingers and toes. And something else, too: an amazing sense of freedom, of release, begins to dance in me. Something extraordinary happened out there. And I came through, and I'm all right. But it's more than *all right*: a feeling too tender and new to put into words.

As I climb up the path from Beady Pool, I sense how late it actually is. There are no lights from the pub, or from any of the houses on this side of the island. I've been in the sea for hours.

The bracken and low gorse bushes either side of the small footpath scratch my bare ankles as I pass. A bramble snags my skirt, but I don't stop to untangle it, just tug myself free and walk on, the dripping wetsuit heavy over my arm. Every so often I stop to change arms.

Something—an animal of some kind, snuffles

157

ahead of me. I stop a moment, and the shadow takes shape: a dog. Its eyes shine as it turns its head. I make out the white patches on its fur, the plume of a tail wagging. It's the young dog from the farm.

'Bess?'

She comes towards me, body crouched low, tail wagging, and I reach my hand out to touch her. She starts at the bulky shape I'm carrying, whimpers.

'It's OK,' I soothe. 'Hey, Bess. It's only me.'

Her breath is warm on my cold hand. I smooth her soft back, feel the way her skin is still loose on her frame, the way she quivers as she stands next to me. When I start walking again she falls in behind me, trotting at the same pace, as if she's keeping me company. It's just her and me. Everyone else is asleep.

When we get to the lane the sky seems much darker. Thick clouds have covered the moon and the stars. The air is cool and wind gusts in the trees, shaking the leaves and sending shadows leaping across the lane.

'Don't bark,' I whisper to the dog. 'We don't want to wake anyone now.'

At the gate, I leave her behind. She stands and watches, as if she's waiting for me to go round the house and out of sight before she goes back to the farm.

I dump the wetsuit in a heap in the shed. I'll rinse it out in the morning. There's a hollow sound of something small rolling out over the wooden floor; I bend down to pick it up. It's not a pebble, or a shell. It's hard and smooth and cold in my hand, and perfectly oval. I've already guessed what it is, way before I get up into my room and switch on the light by the bed. Tonight, nothing is a surprise. It's a bead, green spiralled in gold, sea-worn and ancient, made of Venetian glass.

Twenty-five

It's the first thing I see when I open my eyes the next morning, on the window sill where I left it last night. In the daylight the bead looks plainer and less magical, but I know how rare and special it is. All these years of looking and I've never found one. It seems remarkable that it should somehow just be bundled up in the wetsuit like that. Did it wash in with me on a wave, somehow caught up in the wetsuit? Or had the tide already left it on the sand and by some trick of luck, some accident, I picked it up with my towel and wet things as I left the beach last night?

I turn it over in my palm. Hundreds of years old, and it's landed here, in my hand. I rub it with a corner of the sheet, shining the green glass till it's almost good as new. The gold spiral is inside the glass, somehow. Perhaps Izzy will make it into a new necklace for me.

Instinctively, my hand goes up to my neck. There's no necklace there. The string must have broken when I was swimming last night. My talisman necklace has gone for ever, lost to the sea.

Some things get lost, others return. That is how it is: the way of things.

A squall of rain spatters the window. The fine

weather's broken, like Gramps said it would. There'll be no more swimming today.

*   *   *

'It's chilly,' Evie says when I finally come downstairs for some breakfast. 'I'm going to make us a fire, even though it's midsummer!'

She goes to the shed to find wood, and an axe. Just too late, I remember the wetsuit dumped there last night in a sandy, dripping heap.

I find her hauling it out on to the lawn. 'Such a mess, Freya! Honestly! How long has this been here?'

'Only yesterday. I was going to wash it out and I forgot. Sorry.'

Evie's got tears in her eyes. 'It's Joe's. Just for a snap second I thought Joe was still here.'

I put my arms round her, and we stand together in the shed, both thinking about Joe. But something's different for me now, after last night. Some of the sadness has shifted.

Evie sniffs. 'I'm glad you're using it. It's a good thing. We can't go on like this for ever, not touching his things. He isn't here any more, not in the same way, at least. Because in another way he's always here. Everywhere. I see him. Hear him. We all do, don't we?'

'Yes.' It's such a relief, to hear Evie say that.

Evie disentangles herself. 'Which is why it would be a very good thing if your mother would get herself here and face up to it once and for all.' She sounds almost cross.

I don't say anything.

'Give it a good rinse, and hang it up. Does it fit?'

160

'Nearly,' I say. 'Good enough.'

'That'll save us a few quid, then!' She tries to laugh, but it comes out more like a sob.

'Shall I chop some kindling?' I say. It was Joe's job, before.

'Yes.' Evie takes the basket from the hook and fills it with logs to take back in. 'Careful with the axe. Use the chopping block.'

The rain carries on all day. Mid-afternoon, Danny turns up at the door, dripping wet. Evie asks him in. We've both been sitting by the fire for ages, reading. Gramps is still sleeping, upstairs. It's good to have a visitor.

'How was the gig-race?' I ask Danny.

'Fun,' he says. His hair's gone longer and straighter in the rain. His eyes look extra bright. 'We lost. Second to last.'

'We always do,' I say. 'Did you go to the pub, after?'

'For a little while. It got a bit rowdy. I missed you not being there.'

I smile.

'The fire's nice. We're freezing in the tent, and there's no space. So Mum and Dad and Hattie have gone to Main Island. There's nothing to do when it rains, is there?'

'Suppose not. Sometimes Sally opens up one of the barns, for table tennis and stuff.'

Danny kicks off his trainers and they steam gently in front of the fire.

'Want to play a game? Evie and Gramps have loads. Funny old ones, mostly. Like an ancient version of *Trivial Pursuit*. You won't know any of the answers.'

We rummage through the drawer, getting out

board games like *Sorry!* and *Scrabble* and some old quiz. We find a compendium with *Ludo* and *Snakes and Ladders* and *Housey Housey*, and play each one, laughing loads and cheating like mad. At the bottom of the drawer there's the box of *Cluedo* I last played with Joe. Danny hauls it out and begins to set out the pieces.

'Matt and Huw both got hammered, last night,' Danny says. 'They were arguing about Izzy.'

'What about her?'

'I dunno. Huw said something about her Matt didn't like.'

'Huw should keep his nose out,' I say. 'Stop messing things up for people.'

Danny looks at me. 'Sorry.'

'It's OK. Why doesn't he get his own girlfriend? He's good-looking enough.'

'More than Matt?'

I feel myself blush. Keep my head down. 'Pass me the dice, then, Danny.'

My heart isn't in the game. Danny's isn't either. He keeps looking at me, and I can kind of guess why; it's obvious really. Everything would be so much simpler if I liked him like that too, instead of Matt. But I'm beginning to understand it doesn't work like that. You're not really in control, not with this falling-for-people stuff. You don't plan who you're going to fall in love with. It's all random—chance accidents of time and place. People are always falling in love with the wrong person, aren't they?

I don't mean I'm actually *in love* with Matt. It's just . . . well . . . it's hopeless. He's in a different league. And he and Izzy belong together. And I like Danny loads as a friend, just not

162

anything more.

*　　　*　　　*

Evie brings us homemade scones. She's obviously just loving having a boy around the house again. She goes back into the kitchen and sings along to the radio. She hasn't done that in ages. She wants him to stay for supper, but Danny says he's got to get back. His parents don't know where he is.

'Bring them all. They could have a meal here and dry out!'

But Danny's gone shy again. He stutters, 'No, thank you.'

'He's such a nice boy,' Evie says, as he goes out the door. He probably heard her. She probably meant him to. 'Was I very embarrassing, Freya?'

'Yes, of course!' I say, but I laugh, too.

*　　　*　　　*

When Evie takes a tray of supper up to Gramps I go with her and we sit on his bed. We tell him about our day. He listens and smiles, but he doesn't say much.

'I'm tired out,' he says. 'I'll be better in the morning. Tomorrow's a new day.'

It's still raining, quietly. I stand at the open back door, looking out on the sodden lawn. A blackbird's tugging up an earthworm from the damp earth beneath the apple tree. High in the branches, a thrush sings. I know it's a thrush because it sings every phrase three times, and Gramps taught me that. His bees will be tucked up snug in the hive this evening. I wonder whether

Evie's told them about him being ill. You're supposed to tell the bees everything that happens in a family. He's ill, and it's raining, and I'm lonely tonight, but I don't feel terrible like I have done before. There's a kernel of hope growing inside me, little by little, that one day I will feel happiness again. Little bits of happiness, because it's in my nature to be happy. And no one is happy all the time. It's only ever in bits.

'Close that door, Freya!' Evie calls, but she comes to stand beside me in the open doorway and puts her arms round my shoulders. We watch the rain together. A flurry of wind shakes the tree and a shower of tiny green apples fall on the grass.

'It's been a strange sort of day,' she says. 'Gramps says the rain will blow out to sea again tonight and it'll be fine again by the weekend.'

He's usually right, is Gramps. Fine weather for the holiday weekend, then, and for Dad's journey over, and Izzy's return.

'I'll run you a bath, if you like,' Evie says. 'You look tired out. Too much sitting around doing nothing!'

'I'm all right.'

I think of last night, swimming. If she knew!

*   *   *

Upstairs, getting into bed after my bath, I slide out my phone from where I left it under my notebook. There's a message. Two messages, in fact.

Message 1. **Sorry I was out. See you soon? Missing you. Love Mum xx**

She still hasn't got the hang of texting. She spends ages spelling out the words and putting in

164

punctuation and everything.

Message 2 is from Miranda. **RU OK? Lv M**

Nothing from Sam, then.

I stare at the black letters on the little screen, as if they might suddenly all jumble up and rearrange themselves into a different message, from someone else.

I feel strangely flat. Disappointed, I suppose.

So that's that, then? The End.

Huw was right. Sam's not going to help. Even if I phoned again, got to talk to her, there wouldn't be any point. I finally get it: what could she possibly tell me that would make any difference, now?

*   *   *

Wind batters a wet branch of climbing rose against the window glass. In the distance the black rocks of the Bird islands are silhouetted against the dark grey sky. The Bird islands are where Joe's body finally washed up, smashed against the rocks. I make myself think about it. Face it. His skull was cracked, the autopsy report said, but that might have happened long before he reached the rocks. It's just possible he hit his head on the boom as it swung round when the dinghy hit the full force of the wind out in the bay, and the blow was enough to knock him unconscious, so he couldn't swim when the boat capsized.

The islands are uninhabited except by hundreds of sea-birds: gannets and skuas and guillemots, even puffins, some years. You can take a boat trip out to see them after the nesting season is over. To begin with, I couldn't bear to think about it: his limp body turned over and over by the waves, smashing up against the rock face. But it was just his body, like a hollow shell; the real Joe wasn't there any more. The real Joe had broken free, like one of the sea-birds wheeling high in the wind.

Twenty-six

'There's a letter for you, Freya.'

Evie has propped it up against the honey pot on the kitchen table. We both recognise the writing on the envelope.

I take a mug of tea and Mum's letter out into the garden. The rain's stopped but the grass is still sodden, so I go into the greenhouse and drink my tea there, sip by slow sip, among the tomato plants and the red peppers. I can't remember the last time Mum wrote to me. It makes me nervous, seeing the small neat writing in black ink across thick white paper. Has she something she wants to tell me, that she didn't dare say out loud, on the phone? Hands trembling, I pull the pages out of the envelope.

Dear Freya

It was lovely to get your postcard. I'm so proud of you, getting on with island life this summer by yourself. Evie tells me bits and pieces when she phones. I was sorry to hear about Gramps being ill. How is he now? Evie says you are making all the difference to them, being there.

It has been very strange in this rented house with just your dad and me. Lots of time for thinking and talking. We haven't even unpacked all the boxes. It all feels very temporary. I've been to see a possible house for us to buy: smaller than our old one, but with lovely views and a big garden (all a mess, and the house needs lots of work, of course!) and only a walk from the city centre, which you would like. We are both going to see it again tomorrow, I hope. I think it will be a new start for us all. A different house, without all the sadness of our old one.

This next bit is hard to say. Here goes.

I know the way I've been so wrapped up in my own grieving for Joe has been very difficult for everybody, especially you. I'm so sorry I've not been able to help you more, Freya. So very sorry. It's like I've been in the bottom of this deep black well. I'm slowly climbing back out of all that now, bit by bit. It takes a long time, doesn't it? But moving out of the old house seems to have helped me take the first few steps. I have decided to go back to work in September, part-time to begin with, which has pleased your dad no end.

I am missing you so much! We think it would be a good idea for both of us to come over for the holiday weekend. Evie seems to think so, too. So I will see you soon, darling. I thought we might do something to remember Joe, together, on the day. August 25th. As a family. What do you think? I can hardly believe it's been a whole year.

Sometimes it's easier to write things down. I know you'll understand that, my dear, brave daughter.

Dad sends lots of love (he's sitting here in the kitchen with me, having coffee, though he's supposed to be working).

With all my love, Mum

*　　　*　　　*

I read the letter over at least three times. It makes my eyes sting with tears, and my heart aches, reading her words, but I can't help but see all the times she writes that tiny word *we*: Dad and her, together. They are going to look at a house together. They are coming here, both of them. Right then, when she was writing to me, they were sitting together in the kitchen, having coffee.

So much has happened in a few weeks. It's happening for me, here on the island, my heart beginning to mend, and it seems as if it's happening for them, too.

My hand trembles when I finally get down to writing back. I practise in my notebook first, so I don't make mistakes. It seems important to find exactly the right words, but it's so difficult.

Sometimes it feels as if Joe is right beside me. I hear his voice, or I catch sight of him on the rocks below as I go across the cliffs at Wind Down. I dream about him night after night. He is everywhere on the island, because this is a place where he was happy, and felt like he belonged, and that's why it will be good for you and Dad to come here too.

I think about him all the time, but new things happen too. Good things. I've made some new friends, really special friends . . .

If we do something for Joe (What? Say poems? Talk about him? Best memories? Funny memories? Float candles on the water?), I think we should do it in a way that's quiet but not sad. Not too sad, anyway. Nothing complicated: just remembering the real Joe.

But I don't send it. The words stay in my notebook.

Twenty-seven

Friday morning. Danny and I are sitting cross-legged on the grass near his tent, helping his little sister and Rosie and other kids from the campsite make paper lanterns, ready for the party tomorrow night. Sally calls it Lantern Night: she does it every year, in late August, and everyone from the island joins in. People make food, and bring drink, and there's a procession across the island from the campsite to Beady Pool, with everyone carrying lanterns: hand-made, old-fashioned lanterns with real candles in them, hung from hooks on sticks.

So here we are, Danny and me, trying to bend wire into spiral lantern shapes, only it's much more difficult than it looks and most of ours are a bit wonky. Maddie and Lisa's are much neater. We help tear the sheets of coloured tissue paper to stick over the wire. Where you overlap layers of paper you get different colours: that's the idea, anyway. In reality everyone gets glue all over them, and the tissue sticks in all the wrong places, and gets torn, and we keep losing bits as the wind blows, so that the field is littered with coloured paper. Hattie and Rosie have soon had enough. We send them off to pick up the litter, but they don't want to do that either, so Danny and me end up doing everything.

Afterwards, we help Lisa and Maddie carry the

finished lanterns up to the farm to keep them safe.

'They look beautiful!' Sally beams. 'Stick them in the barn till tomorrow. I've put the box of nightlights in there, ready.'

'Seen Matt?' Lisa asks me, as we troop back down to the field.

I shake my head. I haven't seen him for days. I've been keeping my distance. It's easier like that.

'Izzy will be back this afternoon,' I say. 'Perhaps he's gone to meet her.'

*   *   *

Danny and I walk across Wind Down to the maze carved into the turf on the clifftop. He waits while I run round it, clockwise, to the middle and then back again, like I used to do with Joe. Together we climb up the huge outcrop of wind-carved boulders at the far end of the downs, till we are way up high. We look back across the island towards the Sound.

'No sign yet,' I say.

The wind buffets us. We lean into it, to see if it can hold us up. The crossing will be rough again today.

'We could go and wait on the wall,' I say.

'If you want. When's it due?'

'Who knows? The ferry's always late when the weather's like this.'

'Or we could fish?' Danny looks vaguely hopeful.

'You can. Not me.'

I hop down, boulder by boulder, and Danny follows.

*   *   *

We pick blackberries from the hedges round the small fields in the middle of the island. They've plumped out after all the rain, sweet and glossy.

Above the jetty, we sit on the wall to wait for the *Spirit* to come back from Main Island.

'This is where I first saw Samphire,' I tell Danny.

I've told him lots, the last few days. I even told him about me swimming that night, by myself: everything except about Joe swimming with me, holding me up when I was too tired to swim any more. He was cross for ages. 'It's too dangerous,' he said. 'How could you? Imagine if something had happened to you.'

'Are you still worried about your mum and dad?' he asks.

'Not so much now, not after the letter. But it will be a bit weird, seeing them again.'

'I can't imagine it,' Danny says.

'You don't need to. Your parents are, like, rock solid. Anyone can see that.'

'We haven't had anything . . . anything really bad happen, though, in our family. Like you, I mean. You don't know what would happen, then,' Danny says.

'I reckon they'd still be rock solid. They care too much about you and Hattie. It's obvious.'

'Your parents care about you, Freya! The two things don't go together, silly!'

'It was the silences I couldn't stand,' I say. 'The not knowing.'

'Maybe they didn't know either. Maybe there wasn't anything they could tell you, before.'

I slide off the wall and hunt around for an old can or something for us to aim at, like we always used to do, last summer, waiting here. We each

171

collect a pile of stones.

Danny's first shot goes way off.

'Rubbish throw!'

'You do better, then.'

My stone falls short. I try again, a near miss. I've got better at aiming, since last year. Next go, though, Danny hits the can clean off the rock. He goes over to put it back.

'Hey! Boat's coming,' he calls back.

My belly gives a lurch. Any minute now.

The farm tractor-trailer trundles down the lane towards the jetty, Huw at the wheel, ready to take bags and gear back to the farm. He doesn't seem to notice us.

'Can you see them yet?' Danny says.

The *Spirit* chugs across the grey-blue water of the Sound, leaving a spiral of white wake and a cloud of gulls behind.

I've a lump in my throat.

'I'll leave you to it,' Danny says. 'You won't want me hanging around.'

Dear, thoughtful Danny. How could I ever have thought he looked so much like Joe? OK, he's got the same sort of hair, same sort of clothes, but that's about it. Now I've got to know him, I can see how different to Joe he really is. How much he is himself.

*   *   *

I hang back, waiting for everyone to get off the boat, and for Huw and Matt to load the bags on to the trailers. Izzy sees me and waves. Mum and Dad are the last to get off. They carry their own small bags. They stand on the steps where the boat has

172

tied up, waiting. Huw and Matt change places: Huw goes down into the boat to help Dave, and Matt climbs up into the driver's seat on the tractor. Izzy squashes in next to him, already laughing. Matt starts the tractor engine. Huw and Dave untie the boat and cast off, chugging away again over the water.

I watch it all unfolding, waiting for the moment when everyone will have gone but us.

Every arrival on the island is like a kind of new beginning.

Mum and Dad, side by side, stand on an empty quay.

I walk slowly down to meet them.

*   *   *

Gramps comes downstairs for supper. There's roast lamb, and summer pudding made with raspberries and redcurrants from the garden and the handfuls of blackberries we picked from the hedge next to the lighthouse garden, on our way back from the jetty. It's a family meal, a kind of muted celebration.

We talk about what to do, for Joe's day. One year since his accident. We are beginning to talk about him, all of us, at last.

'What about something in the church?' Evie says, as she passes round the potatoes. 'Not religious, but a sort of gathering where we can have readings, and talk about our memories, and have flowers and music.'

'Too like a funeral,' Mum says. 'We don't want all that again.'

Gramps and Dad are quiet while Mum and Evie

bat ideas back and forth.

'No fussing,' Gramps says, eventually. His hand shakes, spilling peas from his fork on to the tablecloth. 'No arrangements and busyness.'

'Perhaps we shouldn't do anything, after all,' Mum says. 'Joe's in our hearts all the time, anyway. We think about him every day, all of us. It's not as if we need anything special to remind us of him.'

'Sometimes it helps,' Evie says, 'to mark the stages. The passing of time.'

'I think it should be outside,' I say. 'At the beach. Candles, floating out on the sea, and we each just think about Joe, in our own way.'

Mum nods, and then Evie.

'Sounds lovely. Simple.'

'That's decided, then.'

*   *   *

The house feels full again. Mum and Dad tramp up and downstairs. They put their bags and coats and shoes in Joe's room. From the doorway I see Evie has moved things round: there's a cream cover on the bed; the shells and things have been cleared off the shelf. It smells different, already.

Later, Mum comes and sits on the edge of my bed. I've been lying there, writing in my notebook about the day. It's just beginning to get dark.

'Don't you want the light on?' she says.

'Not yet.'

'You look amazing, you know?' she says. 'I can't stop looking at you! You've grown up, these few weeks of summer.'

She fiddles with the edge of my blue skirt. 'Where did this come from? It's so pretty. It's not

174

one of Evie's, is it?'

'No. Izzy gave me a pile of clothes she didn't want any more. But this is the only thing I really like.'

'Izzy who we met earlier, on the boat?'

'Her. Yes.'

I show Mum the other clothes, hanging on the hook on the back of my door. Mum takes the orangey-pink dress off its hanger and holds it against herself. Her face is pale above the bright colour, her hair a faded brown, shorter than before.

'Have it,' I say. 'It looks nice. They are magic clothes, anyway. You should see what happens if you put it on.'

Mum smiles. 'What kind of magic?' she asks. 'I thought you'd grown out of all that sort of thing, these days.'

'Change and transformation. *That* kind of magic.'

'Did you get my letter?' Mum asks. 'I thought you might write back.'

'I tried. I couldn't get the words right. But I liked getting yours.'

'Good.'

We're both quiet.

'Were you writing, when I came in?'

'Yes.'

'Your notebook? With the blue cover?'

'Yes.'

'Do you write about Joe, ever?'

'Sometimes. This summer, last summer.'

'Will you show me?'

'Sometime. Perhaps.'

The soft light outside fades to dusk.

'It'll be better, from now on,' Mum says. She reaches out, takes my hand in hers, holds it tight.

We sit close together like that in the darkening room. I lean into her, rest my head against her. She strokes my hair, over and over, gentle as breathing.

Twenty-eight

A small procession of children winds its way down the narrow path to the beach. Above them paper lanterns in all different colours bob and sway on sticks held by each child. The lanterns glow like coloured moons: pink and orange and turquoise and purple.

I've seen it every year since I was small, but still my heart beats a little faster when I see the dancing lights against the dark hillside. Hattie and Rosie are at the front, small figures in pale dresses like people from a long time ago, from a painting.

People on the beach stop talking to watch the procession. It's a moment of magic, the whole beach enchanted for one long night, and this year, when it is midnight, we are going to take the candles down to the sea, and set them sailing on the water for Joe.

Gramps has installed himself grandly in the director's chair which Dad carried all the way for him, now placed firmly in the sand. 'Like Canute!' Gramps keeps joking, to anyone who stops to listen. 'Trying to turn back the tide!' He waves his glass in one hand. Lisa and Maddie are keeping it topped up with brandy. 'Strictly medicinal,'

176

Gramps says. He looks happier than he has done for ages. Dad sits next to him as much as he can, when he's not being hauled off to help Ben's dad and Dave with the barbecue. It's a grown-ups' party, this one, properly organised, and for once Izzy's just a guest. Sally says she doesn't have to start work till Monday.

'It's good to be back,' Izzy says. 'It seemed like I was away ages!' She sits cross-legged next to me on a rug on the sand.

'How was your mum?'

'Fine. She liked her birthday.'

'And your exams?'

'Oh, passed. You know. All fine.' She looks at me with her river-green eyes. 'For what they're worth.'

Things like that don't matter to her.

'So. How've you been, Freya? Did Matt look after you? I asked him to.'

'You asked *me* to look after *him*, Izzy!'

'Did I?' She turns her head, searching for Matt. He's talking to Luke, they're setting up speakers for the music. She turns back to me again.

'And did you? Look after him?'

I laugh. 'No. We went swimming, once. He was working, mostly. He can look after himself, anyway.'

'And Danny boy?'

'What about him?'

'How's he?'

'Just fine! This is his last night. They're going back tomorrow.'

'Will you be sad, Freya?'

'Kind of. I'll miss him. We're good friends now.'

Izzy laughs. 'Just good friends. Honestly, Freya! Listen to yourself.'

177

'I found something amazing,' I say. 'I meant to show you earlier. I found it here, on this beach.'

'A bead?'

'How did you guess?'

'I knew you would, if you kept looking long enough.'

'I wasn't looking, then. It sort of found me.'

'The best way, of course. What's it like?'

'Green glass, with gold spirals. Really beautiful.'

'I'll make you another necklace, if you like. With a proper chain and everything, not string, this time.'

'It broke, the string. I lost the talisman necklace when I was swimming.'

'You didn't need it any more.'

I laugh. 'What *are* you, Izzy? My guardian angel, or a witch, or a fairy godmother, or something?'

Izzy stands up. She shakes out her crazy hair, the braids all combed out so it falls like a crinkly curtain round her shoulders. 'Take your pick!' she says. 'What would you like me to be?'

'Just you.'

'It's funny, isn't it,' Izzy says, 'how everything's changing all the time. Nothing stays still. Look at you. And your mum and dad, too.'

Things get lost and things return.

The music starts up. Izzy twirls round, so her dress floats out.

'Shall we dance?' she says, holding her arms out to me in a mock-old-fashioned way, as if we're about to waltz round a dance floor.

But Matt is already there, one arm round Izzy's waist, spiriting her away to dance with him on the silver sand.

178

*　　　*　　　*

It's like a dream. It's as if I'm watching everything happening, but I'm part of it too. Mum's wearing the orange dress, waiting for the magic to begin, and maybe it will: every so often Dad, talking to Gramps, goes quiet, watching her, a little smile on his face. Evie and Sally start dancing together, larking about. It's almost dark now.

Danny comes over. 'We're off in the morning,' he says.

'I know. I'll come and wave goodbye.'

'Will you?'

'Of course.'

'Here.' He pushes a piece of paper into my hand.

I can just about see it's an email address and a phone number and a postal address in Danny's careful writing, his name printed clearly at the top. He lives in London: it's only an hour and a half away from me by train.

'Thanks, Danny. I'll give you mine tomorrow. Promise.' I hug him, and he looks so surprised and happy I stay hugging him longer than I meant to. And then I find I'm holding his hand, and we stay sitting together like that quietly in the dark, and it seems the most natural thing in the world. Funny, how things just happen.

Above the wine-dark sea, a golden harvest moon rises. On the beach, the paper moons each throw a small coloured circle of light on the sand like an echo. Later, when the moon is high in the sky, we will float the candles on the water. Each small light will sail out bravely across the dark water, bobbing on the waves, its tiny flame flickering and wavering. We'll remember Joe, and watch each

179

star of light float out further and further away, into the darkness.

*   *   *

Accidents happen. Things change utterly in an instant. This is my life now, here, without Joe. You just have to get on with it. Keep hold of the memories. Seize the small moments of happiness.

Good things will happen again. They've already started. This moment, now, I'm happy.

And that's all there ever is: this one moment. And another, and another, and the next one after.